NO PLACE FOR A LADY

MICHELLE HELLIWELL

ISBN: 978-1-9994965-3-1 (ebook)

Cover Design: Selena Blake

Editor: Donna Alward

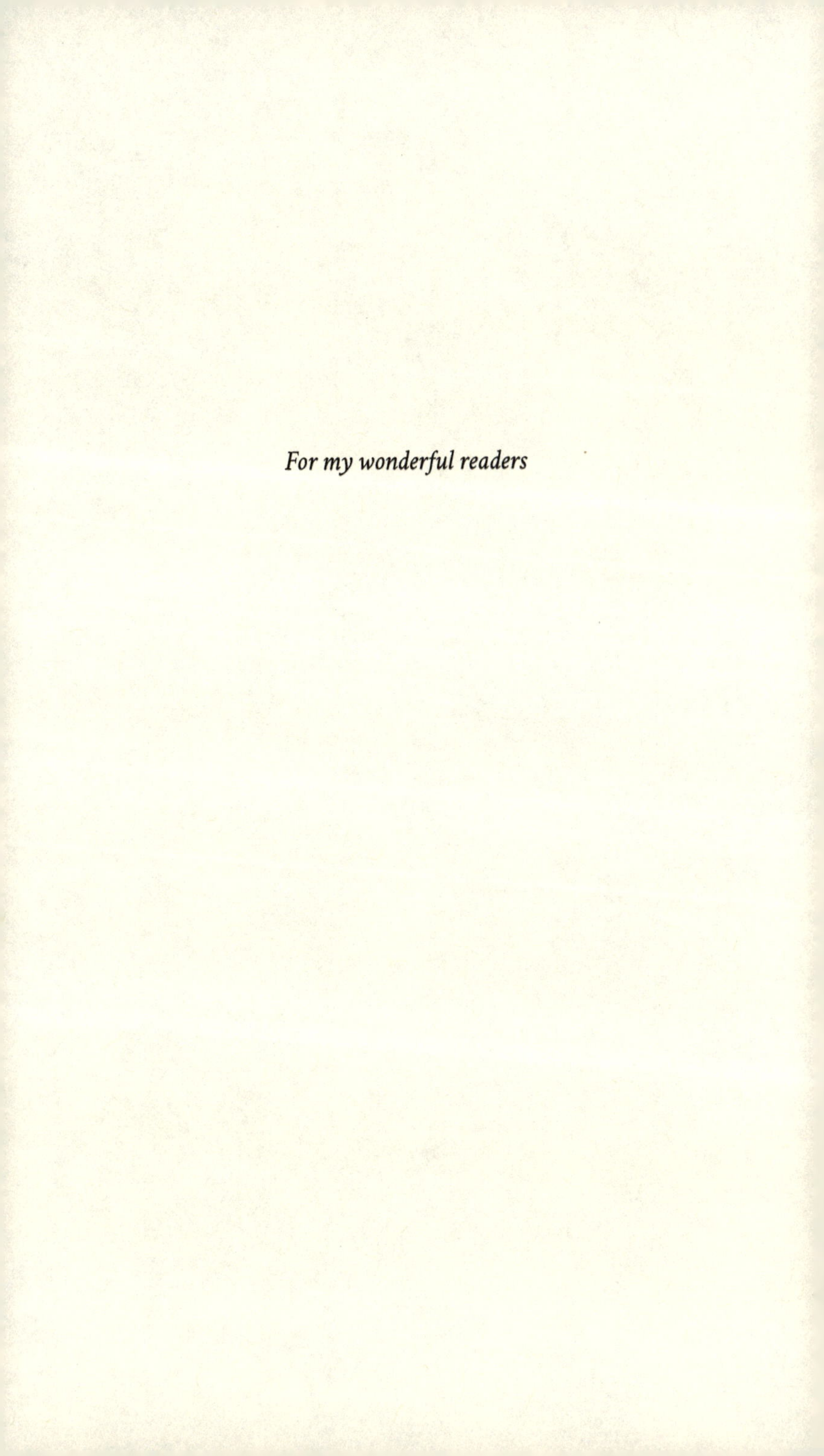

For my wonderful readers

CHAPTER 1

Staffordshire, July 1770

The brooch was at her feet. So close…but *just* out of reach. And thanks to a bodice that had been pulled breathlessly tight, and a cake of a gown with panniers so wide that her skirt spread easily across the width of the garden path, that brooch would remain forever out of reach.

It seemed the perfect metaphor for Lady Sara Whitmore's current circumstances.

A lady does not get engaged everyday, her parents had said when she'd protested the lavishness of the gown. It was critical she make an excellent impression, not only for her intended, Viscount Sharpton, but the cream of English society now gracing Langdon Park. She'd worn her grandmother's favorite shoes, encrusted with Italian crystals, and had drawn the attention of all; the Marquess and Marchioness of Barronsfield, the young Duke and Duchess of Weymouth, and most especially Baron and Baroness D'Anville. No expense had been spared for this lavish affair.

Which was remarkable in of itself, because the Whitmores had no expenses to spare.

And so Sara was trapped, as it were, marrying a wealthy man nearly twice her age. The marriage to Viscount Sharpton would allow Langdon Park to stay with the family, and save her family from the embarrassment of retrenchment, which in the Whitmore hierarchy of sins was perhaps second only to murder.

The sweet scent of gardenia and honeysuckle carried on the warm evening breeze as Sara stood alone in the garden under the shadow of the great house. The windows of the manor were ablaze with light, and the steady din of voices and music revealed a house full to the brim with very important guests. The farcical display only served to remind Sara that, at eighteen, her opportunity to find the person she'd always dreamt of—a worthy man her grandmother told her she was destined for—was over.

Sara picked up the hem of her dress, peered down over the landscape of pink silk brocade that ensconced her body, and gently tapped the brooch with the toe of her shoe. Perhaps if she could find a piece of cane…

"Can I help you, my lady?"

The low, familiar tones of a man's voice caught her attention, driving every other thought from her head. Even before she looked up, her mouth drew up in a smile as a warm, tingly feeling caught in her chest.

She shouldn't even be smiling like this. And definitely not at one of the servants. But Harry Boxford always had that effect on her.

His amber-brown eyes held a hint of mischief that never failed to captivate her. Of course, Harry would have been horrified, no doubt, by the idea that she was captivated by him. By his full mouth, sometimes pulled into that gentle smile. Or the way his smoky brown hair sometimes fell across his eyes when it escaped its queue. Or how his shirt pulled across his shoulders when he was working in the kennels with the dogs, revealing taut, long muscle.

"Harry!" she said, then paused, inwardly groaning at her unchecked enthusiasm. *You are engaged now, Sara.* She swallowed, and forced herself to speak more carefully. "What are you doing here?"

It was a curious question, really. After all, she was the one alone, without a chaperone, wandering the garden while a grand ball in her honor went on without her.

The question hung in the air as the two stood in a curious silence, awareness coursing through Sara. Even though the sun was low in the sky, there was no way to miss the flush of blood rising in Harry's cheeks as his gaze swept over her upper body before meeting her own. Both the bodice and the cut of the gown had been chosen by her mother to display Sara's otherwise modest chest "for maximum effect." Clearly it was having an effect on Harry.

"Heading out for the night watch, my lady," he said at last, lifting his rifle slightly.

As assistant gamekeeper, part of Harry's job was to chase off poachers, and by all accounts, he excelled at it.

"Mr. Barton can't have you working all day and then in the woods all night."

"I'm afraid he can, my lady," Harry replied. "But it's no bother. I like the work."

"You can't work without a rest," Sara protested. "When I am mistress of Langdon Park, I will make sure you have a proper holiday from time to time."

He let out a small laugh. "My lady, poachers don't take holidays."

"Perhaps not. But I think I could spare a brace of rabbits

to allow you a day to yourself. Or a proper night's sleep, at least."

"I enjoy the woods. It's quiet there." His gaze went past her to the windows where the din from the celebrations spilled out into the evening air. "Is that's why you're here? For a bit of peace?"

"You might say that." She'd wanted to escape. But standing here with Harry, her heart racing just a little faster than it had before, she found herself quite inexplicably wanting to be caught.

"Are you certain you don't need help, my lady?" he asked, his eyes narrowing. "It might not be wise for you to be out here alone. Especially if you can barely move."

"I am fine, Harry," she protested. Except for the fact she was about to marry a man twice her age that she'd only met yesterday. "Crowds make me ill-tempered. I merely needed some time to myself. Indeed, I was about to return when you passed by."

Harry's brows knit together as he reached up and rubbed the back of his neck.

"Yes, my lady."

If Sara didn't have to make such an effort to breathe, she would have sighed. Harry's "yes, my lady" had one of a possible hundred interpretations. Given the hint of exasperation in his tone, at the moment "I don't believe you" was the most likely meaning.

"I am well. I promise."

"Your chest is fluttering faster than a bird's wing in a storm," he said, his words edge with was sounded like mild irritation. "You should have your maid loosen your laces before you fall over."

What would it feel like to have his fingers at her back? Sara's gaze dropped to Harry's hands—strong, yet gentle.

Heat wound its way from her chest right down her body, past her belly. *Dear heavens, Sara.*

"A brooch," she blurted out, pointing to the spot near her toes where it lay. "It was my grandmother's. It's right there, but I am trapped in this ridiculous gown and can't bend over. I can't leave it here. Can you help me?"

Could he help her?

He would help her 'til his dying day if he could. But the help she truly needed—to be free of this farce of a marriage her parents were forcing her into—was beyond his ability to give.

It took all of his strength not to feast his eyes on her lush curves. She might have been a viscount's daughter, and he one of dozens of her father's servants, but he was a man, after all. And Sara was the prettiest girl he'd ever laid eyes on. Not that he dare say so.

But he wasn't accustomed to seeing her like this—all trussed up like a bird at a feast—and her discomfort needled him. Lady Sara reminded Harry of a caged bird—agitated, her shallow breaths making her chest rise and fall in an exaggerated fashion.

"Yes, my lady."

He tore his gaze away from her to the ground, where the glint of precious stones caught his eye. There, near the hem of her skirts, lay the object in question—three clear stones, diamonds no doubt, capping a fourth hanging below them that looked to be a field of stars swimming in a milky iridescent stone. Effortlessly he picked it up, struck immediately by the weight of it.

"Thank you!" She reached out with her slender fingers, taking the jewel in her hands. Was it his imagination, or did her touch linger? Awareness shot through him, her earnest smile making him feel warm, as if he'd had too much ale.

He watched her struggle to put the brooch back in place, but the construction of the gown forced her shoulders back and her chest forward, and clearly made it difficult for her to manage. She needed to return to the house. He needed to get to work. And, convincing himself that both of those things were more important than any good sense he should have abided by, he lowered his rifle to the ground.

"May I, my lady?"

She looked up at him, softening, and nodded.

Ignoring her lush breasts, or the scent of honeysuckle on her skin, or the sensation of her body beneath his fingers, he deftly fastened the brooch in place.

"Thank you, Harry," she said.

"You should return to the house, my lady," he said. "You don't know who's lingering in the shadows."

She nodded, her expression hardening into resolve, then walked toward the house. Harry watched her until she walked up the stairs of the great manor, then picked up his rifle and continued on his way. Only a few moments ago, he'd held more wealth in his hands than he might earn in his lifetime. Even if, in his wildest, most forbidden dreams, he and Lady Sara could be together, there was nothing he had that was worthy of her.

When he'd left for his evening's work, stretched and sore after a full day foraging for pheasant eggs, then saving one of the viscount's houseguests from being shot by another rather inept shooter, he'd not been particularly keen on a night in the forests surrounding Langdon Park. But after the sweet torture of being so close to Lady Sara, a long night in the damp woods might be the only cure for his malady.

He had not gotten very far, however, when a curious

sound, like a nervous laugh, caught his attention. He slowed, his ears perking up.

"You don't refuse me, you understan'?" The words were clumsy, spilling into each other, the speaker's tongue clearly dulled by drink. Still, the harshness of them made the hackles on the back of Harry's neck rise.

The nervous laughter that he'd heard a moment ago had changed into something more uneasy. Harry's instincts when on alert, certain he knew who was on the other side of that vile conversation. Turning on the heel of his worn boots, he moved quietly back toward the garden, following the sounds of the voices that were becoming more urgent. Weaving through garden hedges, he found two people standing, their voices animated. One of them was Sara—her back against a hedge, her hands held up to separate her from the black-guard who was busy trying to maul her.

"Fight me all you wan'," the man continued. "It'll be all the more satisfyin' when I get you on yer back, you little bitch."

Harry reached for the drunken lout, a fierce sort of anger coursing through him as he grabbed the man's arms and held them fast behind him. The stink of brandy hung thick in the air, dredging up unwelcome memories of his time spent with his uncle's crew after the death of his parents. Except he wasn't a lad anymore. He'd learned to handle himself—a skill he'd had to use from time to time after he'd taken on the role of watch for Mr. Barton. He could throw a punch just as well as the next man. Still, he hadn't expected to use those skills on a drunken aristocrat in the shadow of his employer's house.

Some men grew jolly with drink. Some grew dull. But this one, Harry could tell, was like his uncle. Fury radiated from him, barely contained in his tight, strangled tone.

"You better have a damn good reas'n fer interrupting a private affair between a gentleman an' his lady."

"Is that what you call it? An *affair?*" Harry drawled with deliberate affectation. "A rather fancy word for forcin' yourself on a lady."

The man managed to wrangle out of Harry's grip, whirling around to face him, his other arm reaching for Harry's throat. Harry replied by grabbing it with both hands, twisting it so that the man had no choice but to swivel in the other direction. Harry swung the bastard around, away from Lady Sara, keeping the pressure on his arm just hard enough to cause him considerable discomfort. It wasn't hard to do. The guttersnipe was a solid man, and no doubt eager to abuse those over which he had power, but definitely not the sort used to being overpowered himself.

"Now, let's say you leave the lady alone, and go back to the house," Harry growled into his ear.

"An' what if I don't?" Even in the dark, his anger was palpable. Add in the drink, and he may have felt invincible. It was a potentially dangerous combination.

"If you don't, I'm going to break your arm so you can't use it to strike anyone again, right?"

"You wouldn't dare!"

"You wouldn't want me to take that dare," Harry growled, a fierce, protective anger growing inside. To make his point, he pulled back harder on the man's arm. Harry wasn't really going to hurt him—not if he could help it. Assault against his betters would send him to prison for sure. And he'd already escaped the noose once. Of course, the son of a bitch didn't know that, and let go an angry, strangled cry.

"Let him go!"

Lady Sara's voice cut through the struggle, but Harry did not lessen his grip.

"Please, Harry," she said, her voice softened. "This is not necessary. Nor helpful."

Harry uttered a low curse under his breath, then released

him—roughly—and tossed him into a nearby boxwood hedge. He turned toward Lady Sara. She sported a different expression than the carefree one he was accustomed to. It was guarded, and she wore her tension in her furrowed brow. Harry's gaze slid over her, looking for any signs of injury.

"Are you hurt, my lady?"

"I am fine." She swallowed deeply, her gaze darting away from him toward the bushes. "You should go on with your duties."

Harry looked around for any signs of the drunken lout, but he was still struggling in the bushes. And from the sound of the retching, losing most of his supper in the process.

"He can sleep off the drink in the bushes," Harry said. "You must return to the house at once. I'll watch until you are safely inside."

Lady Sara nodded, and Harry walked alongside her, the lights from the house silhouetting her face. Her chin was up, he could not help but notice. She seemed none the worse for wear, but he'd long become accustomed to the way she defiantly lifted her chin to mask her emotions.

They wound their way through the hedges of the garden. The size of her skirts made walking beside her nearly impossible. Instead, he followed two steps behind, casually looking over his shoulder to ensure the blackguard who'd pawed at her was where Harry had left him. Soon Lady Sara and Harry reached the house, and she stopped.

"Thank you, Harry," she said, turning to face him, casting a glance beyond Harry's shoulder before returning her gaze to him. Her lips pulled into a tight smile. "I shall be fine. I promise."

"Your father should be made aware of this insult," Harry replied. "That man should not be sheltered under his roof."

Lady Sara shook her head and let go an exasperated, angry sigh.

"Lord Sharpton is not going anywhere, Harry. I'm going to marry him."

CHAPTER 2

Sara lay in her bed, idly rubbing her temples with the tips of her fingers in a vain attempt to soothe the dull ache that a poor night's sleep could not completely erase. Somewhere in the distance, the crowing of a rooster announced the dawn, adding further insult to her injury. It seemed a distinctly male thing to do—making a loud, annoying noise to proclaim something that anyone with a decent set of eyes could deduce for themselves.

Light streamed in through the crack in the heavy blue damask that covered her windows. She draped her arm over her eyes, shielding them from dawn's arrival. It was still very early, and the house was quiet after a night of frivolity. Her parents were late risers. It would not be unheard of for her father to use the cock's crow as his signal to retire, rather than wake. By all accounts, he'd been thrilled with the ball and the fact that Langdon Park was bursting with important guests, whose presence provided not only the social proof of Sara's engagement to Lord Sharpton, but also that her parents' efforts at hiding their scandal had been successful. Of course, the house would be emptied again by tomorrow.

A bankrupt viscount could only afford to feed and fuss over so many important people for so long. Of course, all her parent's woes would be ended when Sara married, and no one, her parents assured her, had to be the wiser. Lord Sharpton had assured her parents of his discretion in the matter of their financial state, which was, along with his considerable fortune, a mark in his favor.

A lifetime with Lord Sharpton in exchange for her family's future. It was a bargain, her parents had told her, but she could not help but wonder about the true cost of the marriage. Sara sniffed as she recalled the cloud of stale brandy and perfume that had assaulted her senses as he'd pulled at her gown.

Her mind wandered back to last evening, cataloguing all that had happened, from the first approving looks of Lord Sharpton as he'd taken her to the dance floor as their engagement was announced, to the applause as they'd danced their first set. Lord Sharpton's manners had been, if not entirely pleasing, courteous. And her parents had been pleased with Sara's conduct through the entire evening—an occasion so rare that it may have rested in the same classification as a sighting of unicorns and fairies.

The cock crowed again, pulling Sara out of her reverie. She threw off her coverlet and sat up in her bed, a pall of dread settling on her shoulders like a lead-lined cloak. Love was the realm of folk tales and fairy stories, and there was always some ghastly business involving ogres and beasts and giants. In the real world, daughters married who they were told to marry, and that was the end of it. She may not have a choice to marry Lord Sharpton, but perhaps she could console herself with finding ways to avoid him. If he liked London, she would long for the country. Indeed, Langdon Park had over a hundred rooms. Surely she could find a way to avoid sharing space with him.

Swallowing back the dread that had caused a lump in her throat, Sara sprang from the bed and shook off the chill of the morning air. She crossed her arms, hugging herself, as she pushed away the loathsome thought of Lord Sharpton touching her.

In its place was a different, much more pleasant thought. The gentle, protective presence of Harry Boxford. The very memory of him tossing Lord Sharpton into the boxwoods made her smile. And wince. It was a dangerous business for a man of Harry's standing to interfere with a member of the peerage.

Harry was by no means a huge man but he stood nearly a full head above her, his body hardened by exertion. Not that she should have noticed. But since he'd arrived last summer, she'd found herself giving in to the compulsion to visit the kennels or walk past the rabbit warrens for no other reason than the chance to spend a few moments with him.

She could picture him even now, in amongst the hunting dogs and the oily rags used to polish the hunting rifles, his skin bronzed by the sun, fussing over guinea fowl in a manner that almost made Sara envious. His body might be hard, but his voice and his looks were anything but. His eyes were a golden brown, like the rich color of spirits, and it seemed to Sara they did all the speaking for him. For he rarely said much to her—with his voice, at least. Two simple phrases formed ninety percent of his communication with her. Indeed, he may have spoken with her more last evening than in the last half a dozen talks they'd had combined.

"Yes, my lady," was the phrase he'd used with her most often. Sara smiled at the broad, exaggerated sound of the word "lady" on his tongue. He'd come from Essex, she'd learned. Of course she had to guess that—and when she'd guessed Suffolk and Hampshire, his reply had been the other phrase, "No, my lady."

Except for last night. He'd spoken with her—voicing his concern for her well-being, and taking Lord Sharpton to task for his conduct. Of course, he'd used more than his words to show his displeasure with the viscount, a man leagues above him in rank and consequence. But there was nothing about what Harry did for her last night that was inconsequential. Her heart squeezed, a curious sort of ache spreading in her chest. It wasn't happiness. It wasn't quite sadness either. It was almost…resentment. Which was silly on the whole, to resent being married. This is what happened to the daughters of the gentry, titled or otherwise. She'd never really believed in love. She'd never watched two people who were married actually enjoy being in each other's company. Never once had she'd seen her father or mother looking to a doorway in anticipation of the other, or watched their faces light up when they talked. No lingering looks.

Her toes curled on the rich Turkish rug at her feet—another luxury that would have to be sold, she'd overheard her mother say, if "that girl" didn't marry Sharpton. Candlesticks, jewelry, rugs—all would have to be sold if the Whitmore family couldn't find a way to fill the coffers.

She took in a deep breath as the tightness across her chest grew, then padded to the window and opened the sash, in the hopes that a few breaths of morning air would revive her head and raise her spirits. The sky was awash in blue, orange, and gold which hinted at the promise of sun just below the rolling Staffordshire peaks. Mists settled into small valleys and hovered just below the trees. Birdsong broke the silence.

Sara took in the stillness as a tonic. Perhaps Sharpton was a night owl, like her father. Perhaps, if she was very lucky, she might see him no more than an hour a day—except for when he would come to her for bedding. Disgust slithered down her spine, but she straightened and tossed the sensation aside. She could survive that. And perhaps, once she'd borne him a son or two, he would leave her well enough alone and take up with a mistress. Then, she thought, momentarily buoyed by that faintest glimmer of hope, she might find a way to make herself happy.

The cheerful yip of a dog rose from below, drawing Sara's attention away from her rather moribund wool-gathering. She paused, looking for the source of the noise when it happened again. But this time it was followed by another sound...a gentle bit of laughter and a low voice that rolled over the landscape, unimpeded by the normal cacophony of sounds that filled Langdon Park in the middle of the day.

A figure appeared out of the mists. A male figure, surrounded by a small herd of dogs. A herd? Sara wasn't at all sure what one called a group of dogs. But Harry Boxford would. And it was Harry she saw, walking in long strides across the field, the dogs running alongside, tails wagging madly, as if he was leading them to some kind of doggy nirvana.

Sara's headache evaporated at the sight of him, replaced by yearning that made her happy and melancholy all at once. She went to her wardrobe, pulled out a heavy *robe a chambre* and threw it over her shift. It was scandalous to go without a corset, but she was far less exposed in the heavy layer of light blue damask that fastened just below her chin that the dress she'd worn last night. Besides, no one would see her. Except Harry.

Heavens Sara, he's a gamekeeper.

And not even that—an *assistant* gamekeeper. Ladies did not call out to assistant gamekeepers. But it couldn't hurt to say thank you to the man who'd preserved not only her dignity, but perhaps her virtue, could it? After all, she was about to spend a lifetime with a man who cared about neither.

That sensation came on her again. A heaviness. Of being trapped. And there was only one balm she knew to ease it.

A LOW MIST hugged the ground as Harry walked along the sprawling eastern lawn of Langdon Park. After a long, restless night, his last duty before attempting to steal a few hours sleep was to exercise the dogs. Sheer outrage at the events of last evening had managed to keep Harry going through most of the night. Every time he thought about that bastard touching Lady Sara, a fresh rush of anger flowed through him. But after a long night in the woods on watch, all he wanted was to climb into his bunk and slip into sleep.

"Good morning, you beautiful boy!"

The bright sound of Lady Sara's voice broke through his fatigue.

Beautiful boy? At first, he thought he'd imagined it. But there she was, as fresh and beautiful as a bluebell in spring, crouching down and cooing at one of his spaniels, who repaid her enthusiasm by nuzzling her hands and eagerly accepting all the affection she provided. He sucked in a quick breath, and chided himself for being even remotely envious of a bloody dog. But he was. Her golden brown hair was tied back in a plait loosened from a night's sleep and draped over one of her shoulders, a pretty little ribbon tied around the end. What would it be like, he wondered, to pull that ribbon free, and have it cascade down her back? Or better yet, to run his hands through it—

Steady on, Harry. You aren't fit to touch her.

His fatigue a distant memory, he put his fingers to his lips and let go a short, sharp whistle to get the dog's attention. It was back at his side in seconds.

Lady Sara pulled herself to her feet, which he couldn't help but notice were bare under her long blue robe. The sensation—really, what was so bloody delightful about feet—knocked him off kilter. Because then he was thinking about her legs, which were probably also bare, and shapely no doubt, and—

"Good morning, Harry."

He nodded, pulling his attention back where it should be, and his mind out of the gutter. Touching his fingers to the brim of his straw hat by way of salute, he acknowledged her address the only way he could.

"My lady."

What in the hell was she doing here, out on the side lawn, with nothing between them but a layer of fancy blue fabric and, God help him for imagining it, the thinnest of linen shifts?

Damn it. Harry was always at war with himself over Lady Sara. When he'd arrived at Langdon Park, he'd been eager to prove himself. Eventually, he might earn Mr. Barton's position, or one like it in another household. But every moment he spent in Lady Sara's presence, and every yearning he had for her when she was not, put that future in jeopardy. She always seemed to be there, in the kennels, walking along some wooded path. And while there was some dark corner of his soul where he would allow himself to imagine, just for a moment, that she had anything but the most inconsequential of feelings for him, it was far more likely that Lady Sara had been simply lonely and looking for something akin to companionship. It could hardly be anything more.

"I just wanted to thank you, again, for your service to me last evening." Her cheeks were pink from the chill, and though her eyes were wide and cheerful, a subtle tension along her jaw that tightened her smile and betrayed her nerves.

"Yes, my lady."

"Harry." She threw her hands in the air, clearly exasperated. "We have been friends for over a year. Can you not say more to me than yes, my lady?"

A knot tightened in Harry's gut. Could he not say more to her? He had a litany of things to say—but where would he begin? Perhaps he would start with "you have the prettiest eyes I've ever seen," then move on to "you make a funny little snorting sound when you laugh," and finish with "how in the hell could your parents let you marry such a lecherous bastard?" But he couldn't say any of those things. It was not his place. Especially if he wanted to keep his job. Too much had been sacrificed for him to throw that away.

Instead, he cast an eye past her, toward the house. He was not the only servant up at the crack of dawn. Intelligence of that kind travelled through the downstairs like leaves on an October wind. And if that whoreson of a betrothed discovered her with him, Harry's future at Langdon Park was non-existent.

"I shouldn't be speaking to you, my lady," he replied, barely contained exasperation edging his normally calm demeanor. "Especially when you're in your night clothes. Mr. Barton would have me turned out before breakfast if I was caught."

"He wouldn't, because I wouldn't allow it," she replied, her chin up in that vaguely self-mocking expression she sometimes wore.

He looked away for a moment, his mouth pulling in a tight line as he scratched the back of his neck.

"It's true," she insisted, her voice softening, as she idly toyed with the end of her braid. "You're a hero. You can't be dismissed."

"And when you are married to the man I threw into the bushes?" he said at last, fatigue wearing down his ability to hold his tongue. "I'm not so certain he was pleased with my heroics."

"I—" She stepped back, faltering for the first time. She cast her eyes to the dogs, but her mind seemed elsewhere, as if she was groping for a reply. She quickly turned back to him. "It was evening. Twilight. Even if he knew who you are, he would never recognize you."

"It is daylight now," he replied, an edge of frustration edging into his voice. He nodded curtly to the windows of the manor house.

"You don't think…" she began, her eyes wide before she glanced quickly over her shoulder.

"Your husband-to-be has his own servants about," he said, his voice low. "He might be sleeping off his drink, my lady, but they are stirring. And watching."

"How do you know?"

"That is what a servant does, my lady. Watch to see what is needed, and respond."

"And what do you think I need?"

The dare in her voice was unmistakable. But he could not rise to it. Though, by God, he wanted to. His gaze rested on her mouth, and he wanted nothing more than to take her by the shoulders and put his lips to hers, to draw his tongue along the curve of her mouth, and taste the bounty he knew lay there. But it was not his place.

Instead, he turned and walked away.

CHAPTER 3

*L*ater that afternoon, Sara sat in the drawing room with her mother and several other ladies, attempting to focus on the fireplace screen she was embroidering. The steady rhythm of her stitches, and the movement of her needle through the stretched fabric, calmed her. Breakfast had passed, and Lord Sharpton had not made an appearance. Neither had her father. Their absence had been noted, most especially by the outspoken Baroness D'Anville, but Sara had been more than relieved not to have to face Lord Sharpton after that awkward encounter last night.

"Lady Sara," their butler said in a steady voice, "you are required by his Lordship at once."

Sara pressed her lips tightly together to staunch the sigh in her throat. So much for relief.

She set her needlework aside and followed the butler to her father's study, where she was greeted by her father and Lord Sharpton. Lord Sharpton, to her utter surprise, came to her at once in long, confident strides. The pace at which he crossed the floor made Sara not at all confident, especially after last night. On instinct, she stepped backward. Whether

20

her intended noticed her reaction, she could not say. He bowed deeply and took her hand in his. The side of one cheek bore a purple mark and small cut on his right cheek bone.

She stilled, unsure where to look. *Did Harry do that?* He would be finished for certain if that was the case. Not that Lord Sharpton didn't deserve it.

Sara didn't know whether to remark on it or not. Lord Sharpton's manner, in her experience, could be calm and smooth, and then, when fuelled by several bottles of brandy, boorish and spiteful. Presently, his smile was so genuine, his countenance so sincere, it was difficult to reconcile this with the man who'd pawed at her gown and called her unspeakable names when she would not submit to him.

"Lady Sara," he said, taking her hand in his and kissing it. "My heart is troubled and I beg you to end my suffering."

Sara blinked, wanting to pull her hand away from his mouth. "Your…suffering?"

He looked up at her, his icy blue eyes made less so by his expression of repentance.

"You cannot know how my heart aches, and how much it pains me to think of what happened last evening."

"I—" Sara took a quick glance at her father, who stood watching them, stone faced. Lord Sharpton seemed genuine in his apology, but she had little experience with men of any kind, and even less of his ilk. He was a wealthy, powerful man who held favor with the king. Still, there was something about him that put her on her guard. Once upon a time, her grandmother had told Sara to find a man worthy of her. By society's standards, Lord Sharpton was everything a girl could hope for.

Her eyes slid over the purple welt on his face. He'd hardly been worthy of her last night.

Lord Sharpton watched her expectantly. Sara turned her

lips up in a tentative smile, well aware of the role she needed to play. An unwelcome, but increasingly all-too-familiar sensation spread across her chest. She breathed in deeply in an attempt to remind herself that she wasn't, in fact, trapped —though it very much felt that way.

"It was nothing," she replied, mostly to convince herself. She let out a breath and smiled widely, all the while aware of her father's piercing gaze. Never had he paid as much attention to Sara as he had since the announcement of her engagement. The entire wellbeing of the family depended on her conduct. Still, she couldn't help but wonder what would have been different if Lord Sharpton was under similar scrutiny. "Indeed, it is forgotten."

Not really.

"Excellent." His smile froze, then he stiffened slightly and backed away, clasping his hands behind his back. He paced to the window, and turned his glance from Sara to her father. "Still, something must be done about the vicious assault last night."

Sara's smile stalled, her gaze darting between Lord Sharpton and her father. Had she not just forgiven him?

"Agreed," her father said. "I am most grieved by it, Lord Sharpton. Trust me that I will have it taken care of immediately."

"We can discuss the particulars once Lady Sara has departed," Lord Sharpton replied. He smiled at her, though the warmth of it failed to reach his eyes. "This does not concern her. This is far too crass a conversation for such a delicate lady."

Sara wanted to laugh out loud. Too delicate? Lord Sharpton had clearly not concerned himself with her delicacy last night.

"With respect, I was present. And—" *Assaulted,* she wanted to say. She brightened. "—it is in the past. All is forgiven."

"For you, perhaps," her father said. "But not for Lord Sharpton. We must address his attacker."

"*His* attacker?" The words tumbled out of Sara's mouth before she could stop them, surprise having loosened her tongue.

Her intended's countenance became an infuriating mix of condescension and irritation. "Perhaps the intensity of the situation has blocked the incident from your memory. Or perhaps you were gone by then. I do not recall."

You were foxed. It is remarkable you remember anything.

"My dear, Lord Sharpton was attacked by one of my own staff. I cannot abide it. A common laborer, attacking a peer! It cannot be borne. I have agreed to assist him at all costs," he replied. Her father was upset, though, clearly, not because of the transgression against her. "While Lord Sharpton was most eager to apologize in my presence for whatever happened between you—a gesture that was hardly necessary—the simple fact is that you were present and may be able to identify the attacker without having to turn out the entire staff in front of a household of guests."

Lord Sharpton's attacker. Her stomach lurched and an uncomfortable heat pricked along the back of her neck.

Harry.

"I don't recall who it was, Father," she said at last. "It was twilight, and there was heavy shadow."

Her father walked out from behind her desk, standing beside Lord Sharpton.

"Are you quite certain? I realize that as a whole the underclass is unremarkable, but there must be something that might have distinguished the blackguard. They might have been particularly large, or brutish in appearance."

"I—I just—" Sara swallowed. She wasn't used to this sort of scrutiny from anyone, and most especially not her parents. Heat rushed into her face, and she swallowed as she tried to tamp down a growing sense of panic. "It was a man. But I couldn't say after that."

Lord Sharpton made no noise, but the cold threat in his stare sent a needle of fear straight through Sara's chest. She paused and swallowed deeply, knowing she had to choose her next words very carefully.

"Perhaps she does not recall," Lord Sharpton interrupted, his tone clipped and business-like. "The shock might have been too much for someone of her delicate constitution." He turned his gaze to her, his stare raking over her face as his lips twisted with the smallest hint of a sneer. "I am certain she would never intentionally shield a criminal. Even if she is familiar with him."

Familiar with him. Despite the July heat and several layers of petticoats, a chill slithered down Sara's back. Lord Sharpton was testing her.

"Indeed, I believe I heard her speaking to him by name. But perhaps I could have been mistaken."

Dear heaven. He knew she was lying.

"There was someone there," she said stiffening her spine, daring to take his test and pass it. But panic warred with her determination to answer his challenge, and her voice rose. "But on my life he intervened only to stop what he thought looked like a perilous situation. I am positive he had the best of intentions to protect me."

"Whatever his intentions, the assault against Lord Sharpton, your betrothed, was the result. I take this as an attack against this house and this family," her father replied, clearly indignant. "Do not further insult me or Lord Sharpton by shielding him. It does you no credit."

Sara blanched at the stinging rebuke. But it was also already entirely possible that Lord Sharpton was perfectly aware of who had struck him last night. And perhaps that she'd been out on the lawn just after dawn, talking to Harry.

Harry had warned her, hadn't he? It would only make it worse for the both of them if she lied about it.

"Harry Boxford, Mr. Barton's assistant, intervened on my behalf because he assumed—wrongly—that my safety was being threatened." She looked past Lord Sharpton to her father, silently imploring him, just once, to listen to her. "As I said, I am confident that this was a terrible misunderstanding."

Her father brightened almost immediately upon her speaking, and for a moment, he almost seemed pleased with her.

"Harry Boxford you say. Excellent." He waved at her with a dismissive gesture. "You may return to your company. I will have this matter dealt with immediately."

Harry would be fired, she knew. Without a letter of recommendation. After all his hard work, he would be tossed out with only the clothes on his back and without the wages he was owed—which were probably several months' worth, knowing the straits the family were in. But given Lord Sharpton's vehemence last night, it was perhaps a forgone conclusion. And better for the both of them. Though it did not feel at all like it.

Sara turned to her father, trying to keep her expressive face neutral.

"Shall I have word sent to Mr. Barton, Father?"

"Why ever for?" he said, his words impatient.

She paused, confused by the question. "So you can inform him of Harry Boxford's dismissal."

"Dismissal? Such a violent action is an affront to my honor, Lord Sharpton's, and by extension, your own. I will not have someone in my home humiliated in such a grievous manner by a common brute." He looked past her to Lord Sharpton. "I have sent for the magistrate."

A pit opened in Sara's stomach. "The magistrate?" she

asked, her voice a breathy question. Lord Sharpton's eyes locked on hers.

"I am certain attempted murder against a peer is a capital offence," her father continued, his ardor for his wounded pride in full display. "He could hang for it."

"Hang?" Sara said, her voice pitched high by the unwelcome shock.

"Now, now." Lord Sharpton's voice was calm and low. "There is no need to bring Lady Sara such distress. Lock the blackguard up for a time, my lord, and let the magistrate do his work. A little time in the stocks or a week in a cell might do wonders to straighten him out. And allows us time to focus on preparations for our upcoming wedding. Does this sound amenable, my dear?"

She looked over to him and smiled, desperately wanting to believe the calm, reassuring temperament he'd adopted. Perhaps, by some miracle, Lord Sharpton would be reasonable, but Sara was not given to believing in miracles. Showing him even a hint of the riotous emotion twisting her insides would make things worse for Harry. Screwing up all of her fortitude, she simply stood and forced herself to smile sweetly, determined not to push the matter further. She laced her fingers together as she tried to collect her thoughts. She had to go find Harry and warn him. She had no idea if it was better for him to run, or to stay and take Lord Sharpton's punishment. But at least if she could get to him, he could decide.

She didn't have a choice. She had to marry Sharpton.

But she could choose to save Harry.

CHAPTER 4

_H_arry lay in his bed in the kennels, his body heavy with fatigue, a woman on his mind. And not just any woman, of course. A woman with bright hazel eyes and a smile that made him feel, somehow, like more than an assistant gamekeeper whose greatest aspiration was to remove assistant from his title and perhaps one day afford a pair of boots with soles thicker than paper.

The yipping of dogs in the kennels pierced the otherwise quiet early afternoon. He stretched, the muscles in his left shoulder so tight they strained against the movement. He was only one and twenty, but he'd be old at thirty at this rate. His father had been a big, strong man—a blacksmith, with shoulders so wide that doors did not seem to be made for him. But he'd been a gentle soul, working hard, and had not complained for it. Harry tried to channel that reserve now.

It had been a much more fruitful night than Harry had anticipated. He'd caught not one, but two poachers, who were clearly emboldened by the grand gathering at Langdon Park. The men he'd caught were professionals, rather than locals trying to fill their larders. Harry had been a professional once upon a time, reared by one of the meanest and best, and all before he'd sprouted hair on his chest. After spending half the bloody night finally convincing the gaoler to take them into the overcrowded lock-up, he dragged himself back to the kennels and saw to the dogs. He'd been bone weary until his encounter with Lady Sara, which had brought every part of him alive.

Every part of him.

But that particular frustration was not the only sensation that robbed him of sleep. The encounter with Lady Sara's fiancé last evening churned in his gut. Harry should have been less rough with the slobbering drunk of a lord, but both the man's heavy-handed manner with Lady Sara and those disgusting words he'd used to describe her had brought Harry's blood to a boil. He would have no choice but to raise it with Mr. Barton today. Perhaps nothing would come of it, but if it did, he didn't want what happened to cast a shadow on elder gamekeeper. The man had his own cares at the moment. Still, after another fruitful night of keeping Langdon Park's deer and pheasants safe, Harry hoped he had proved himself worthy of a reprieve.

There had been tension over the past few days on the estate. Viscount Sharpton had brought some of his own people with him. It was common knowledge that Langdon Park was not entailed, which left Lady Sara in the unusual position of heir. No doubt Sharpton was surveying the property that would essentially be his on the death of Viscount Whitmore. From the house to the stables, they were there to assess and report. Sharpton, it seemed, liked to keep a keen eye on his property.

"Harry."

The sound of Lady Sara's voice cut through Harry's reverie. At first, he thought himself dreaming, but the gentle shaking of his shoulder and the light scent of honeysuckle were too real for it to be otherwise.

"Harry! Get up!"

He started, taking a quick intake of breath as he sat and looked over his shoulder. There was Lady Sara, her blue-green eyes wide and rimmed with worry. In a swift moment, he pulled himself to his feet.

"Yes, my lady," he replied, half acknowledgement, half question, and otherwise too stunned to see her here to say much more.

"You have to leave at once," she replied. "Lord Sharpton is bringing the magistrate to have you arrested."

Bloody hell.

"You have to go, my lady," he said.

"Are you not listening to me?" she asked, clearly impatient with him. "My father is furious. He wants to see you in prison. Lord Sharpton promises to be more accommodating, and maybe he will, but I wanted to warn you."

Harry's scar itched on his hand, and a sinking sensation tightened across his throat. She was in danger, being here, with him. He already had one soul on his conscience. He'd be damned if he'd have another.

"Go."

She blinked, confusion crinkling her brow. Harry realized it was probably the first time she'd ever heard him speak in such a tone. The first time he'd ever given her what was tantamount to an order.

"Harry—"

He turned away from her and went to the window, looking for any sign of the magistrate or Mr. Barton. It would do Lady Sara no favors to be found here with him, and for him? It would be his end.

"It will do neither of us any good if you are discovered

here," he said, deliberately fixing his gaze to the outdoors even as he sensed her move even closer.

"You're not going to be discovered," she said in that aristocratic way of hers. Normally he found it charming, that sense of composure she had. It was never haughty, but rather the self-assurance of a girl who had been raised never to fear for her next meal or a warm bed. The assurance that came from knowing her words would be heeded simply because of who she was. But as much as he found Lady Sara bewitching, there was much about the world she had to learn. Like there were far too many people in the world prepared to sacrifice your neck to save their own.

"And why is that?"

He heard a curious rustling sound behind him, and he turned to find Lady Sara grabbing his canvas sack and shoving his belongings into it. He turned away from the window, but spared himself a final glance, and his stomach dropped.

"Because you're leaving before they can catch you," she said. "If you leave now, there will still be—"

Harry turned away from the window, his heart racing as he reached for the sack in her hands, his fingers brushing up against hers as he did so. Awareness shot through him, cutting through the urgency but for a few seconds.

"He's coming, my lady. You have to leave."

"What about you?"

"I will look after myself like I always have, my lady. I'm not your responsibility."

Her mouth dipped into a frown, then settled into a tight line. "I will fix this, I promise."

Harry nodded, knowing full well that even if she believed it, he knew better.

"Yes, my lady."

She disappeared, sneaking out through the door at the

rear of the kennels. When the telltale sound of the door creaking on its hinges reached his ears, Harry let out a breath of relief.

Relief turned to apprehension at the sound of footsteps approaching the kennels. Harry didn't wait for them to come to him. It was pointless to put off the inevitable.

A small gaggle of men stood before him, crowding his tiny apartment. Mr. Barton was among them, looking distinctly uncomfortable in his own skin.

"That's him. That's the man."

Harry swallowed, recognizing Viscount Sharpton's voice. It was much harder now, the messy slurred outrage replaced by a colder, detached anger. But it was the words, not the tone, that spawned the uncomfortable heat prickling up the back of Harry's neck. The last time Harry had heard that phrase—"that's him"—he'd been arrested. He was thirteen. Poaching for food and to satisfy his uncle's black market dealings.

Sharpton pushed past his own men, moving toward Harry with all the confidence of a man who had the whims of the world at his fingertips. He wore a sneer and the ruddied cheeks of a man who spent far too much time with drink. At his side were the magistrate and two large fellows, hired goons to ensure that the magistrate didn't have to break a sweat catching up with Harry when he ran.

But he wouldn't run. Wouldn't give Sharpton the satisfaction. Maybe, just for a moment, he entertained the notion that these gentleman just wanted to ask him some questions. But experience had taught him differently. Trusting in other people's motives was for fools. The last time he'd trusted anyone, he'd been tossed in prison and waited for the hangman's noose.

That's him.

"Harry Boxford," the magistrate began, his voice dispassionate, "you have been accused of striking Lord Sharpton, causing him bodily injury."

"Aye," Harry said, casting his gaze at the magistrate. "Only because he was attacking a lady."

Lord Sharpton's gaze narrowed. "A lie."

"'Tis the truth. He was forcing himself on her. And when she resisted, he was prepared to strike her," he said.

"You violently pushed me into the bushes," the viscount said.

"When a man's as drunk as you were, it is hardly a chore."

Somewhere in the back of his mind he could hear his uncle's voice. *Stop flapping your lips, you idiot.*

Harry turned his gaze back to Mr. Barton and the magistrate. He knew he didn't have a chance in hell, but he could not let all his hard work go to ruin.

"Barton, you know I would never attack a man unarmed, and I'm not fool enough to go after a gentleman. My job is to protect what is Lord Whitmore's," he said. "And we both know there is no one on this estate better at it than I."

"You protect fowl, deer and rabbits," Mr. Barton said, clearly unwilling to tread on the toes of a man who might someday be his employer. "Not his Lordship's daughter."

Harry shook his head. It would be his word against that of a peer. He knew bloody well on which side of justice he would fall.

"Harry Boxford," the magistrate began, as blandly as if he was ordering a tray of sandwiches, "you are being held for charges for attacking Viscount Sharpton. Lady Sara herself identified you to us as the assailant."

Harry blinked at the words, disappointment striking him in the gut. *Of course, you bloody fool.* Regardless of her smiles, or the hours they spent in quiet conversation, or the way she looked at him that made him feel like he was so much more than a man hired to clean up after dogs and chase away poachers, he was at best a pastime for her.

Ladies who had affairs with stable boys and gardeners were all well and good in folk tales, but in real life—where his very presence wasn't to be acknowledged and direct eye contact was in many cases forbidden—it never ended well. Harry Boxford was no prince in disguise.

Perhaps guilt had brought her to warn him in the end, but it was nothing more than that.

"You'll be held at the gaol until the assizes," the magistrate droned on.

"I only pulled him off a lady," Harry insisted, trying to sound nonchalant, while inside, an old terror welled at the magistrate's words.

"You struck me, you piece of filth. Struck one of your betters. If I were you, I'd keep that mouth of yours shut." Sharpton grabbed him by the shoulder and sent a fist into his gut, forcing Harry to double over. As he swallowed back the pain, he was taken by the shoulders, and felt Sharpton's foul breath at his ear. "I told her I'd ask for leniency. Lock you in the stocks. But I know about that mark. You won't escape the gallows twice."

A blinding pain on the side of Harry's temple was the last thing he recalled before everything faded into darkness.

CHAPTER 5

*H*arry's eyes fluttered open, his body aching from head to toe, and for a moment, he felt strangely out of time and place. It took painful moments for his senses to unravel the tangle of sights, smells, sounds, and touch that surrounded him.

Dim light. Musty damp. Unearthly quiet. Hard stone.

Panic gripped him, keeping his body in one place as memories came roaring back of that fetid stinking trap of a prison he'd been flung into as a lad. He'd thought he was going to die—either by the rope, or disease, or worse. And he would have, if it were not for Paul Jones. Jones, a swarthy Welshman who'd worked with Harry's uncle, and had been caught in the same raid. He protected Harry fiercely against anyone who'd dared tried to pick on the small, wiry boy. And when it was time to swing, Jones, figuring he'd lived far too long and miserable a life, took Harry's place on the platform that day. If Harry closed his eyes, he could still remember the way the man's feet twitched as he died.

Harry blew out a low shaky breath, fighting to steady himself and focus on the present. He could not rot here. A man had died so he could live. And he would not waste that chance on a whoreson like Sharpton.

The sensation of heavy, cold iron gripping his wrists and his ankles told him he was wearing shackles. But it was too quiet to be the lock-up. No feast of human bodily noises for his ears, and the smell, though hardly roses, was not the fetid reek that came from storing humans like poorly tended livestock.

His gaze was drawn to a solitary window above him, revealing a patch of clear blue sky. He dragged himself to his feet, his movements clumsy from the weight and restricted movement caused by his leg and wrist irons, and moved to the window, which was within easy reach and not shuttered by bars or any other guard to keep him in. When he reached the window, he understood why.

Lush forest, grazing land, and in the distance, gentle peaks filled his view from the solitary window which, he noted, was more than wide enough for him to crawl out if he pleased.

Of course, the forty-foot fall would break both his legs and smash his skull and probably break his neck, making the hangman's noose quite unnecessary.

He turned his back on the window and surveyed the rest of his surroundings. The cell was almost entirely stone. He walked every inch of the floor, testing it, but it was as solid as the walls. The ceiling was at least twelve feet high, supported by thick wooden beams. Bolted to the walls were a few hooks who's purpose were lost to history. In the corner was an old pail to catch his piss.

Harry let go a low, steady breath. This was his bloody fault. All because he couldn't keep to his own business. Since his arrival at Langdon Park, Lady Sara's visits to the kennels had become more frequent, and each time she always managed to find ways to stretch out stolen minutes into hours. They did nothing but talk. Or she talked. He listened, for the most part. And while he should have done more to avoid her, damn it, he found himself anticipating her visits. He'd never thought of himself as lonely. Being alone was safer—less painful. People always wanted to be owed something—taking what they needed and giving blessed little in return. Except for Jones. That man had given everything to Harry. And he'd had to live with that, too.

What happened between the lords of the land and their ladies was not concern, his uncle had once told him. And for once, Harry thought bitterly, the man was right.

He'd hoped with this job that he'd be able to put enough away to get a new pair of boots—or a new-to-him pair at the very least. Now the ones on his feet were probably going to be scavenged by some wretched soul before they cut him down from the gibbet.

Perhaps he wouldn't hang. Perhaps they'd put him in the stocks for a week—or just keep him here for a few days and quietly see him on his way. He'd come close before. Of course, he didn't hang. He'd been lucky.

He gazed down at the faded mark on the inside of his thumb. A letter T—for Thief. He could recall the pain even now, somewhere deep in his memory. But he'd been grateful for it. He'd been marked. One more toe out of line...and there would be no more chances.

His luck had run out.

THE HOURS FOLLOWING Harry's arrest tested every lesson Sara had ever been taught about patience. She'd watched as Harry was clamped in irons and led away, her heart in her throat. Only Harry's warning had kept her from intervening, and she'd learned enough about Lord Sharpton to know that making him look a fool in front of his men would only make things worse.

Whether or not her parents and Lord Sharpton sensed her distress it was difficult to say, but they'd seemed almost conspiratorial in their determination to keep her engaged in one sort of amusement or another for the remainder of the day. There'd been cards and recitals and tea and dinner and more dancing. It had been exhausting, pretending to care about the entire spectacle, especially when one was at the center of it. That night she'd fallen into a restless sleep, anticipating the exodus of guests, including Lord Sharpton, from Langdon Park.

The next morning, Sara stood at the grand entry with her parents, bidding the guests farewell. One after another she smiled and curtsied and accepted well wishes for a future that, while inevitable, was not particularly welcome.

"And here is the lovely bride to be herself."

Sara's daydreaming was interrupted by Baroness D'Anville, bedecked in a dazzling peacock blue Brunswick gown, capped with a delicate fichu. The lady's pursed lips and narrowed gaze dissolved into an earnest smile, but for a moment Sara wondered if she'd dropped the façade of doting hostess.

"It was wonderful to meet you at last," Sara said, and indeed she meant it. Whether it had been her French manners, or her rather *outré* opinions on everything from fashion to politics, Sara had appreciated the baroness's frank assessment of the world around her.

"Likewise," the baroness said in a refined French accent, arched a brow and leaned closer, her voice lowering into an excited hush. "I must know where you acquired those beautiful shoes you wore the evening before last."

Sara smiled. "They were my grandmother's. I believe they

were made for her by a bead maker in Murano. They are one of a kind."

"They were stunning," she smiled in approval. "As was the brooch you wore. A moonstone, I believe?"

Sara nodded, amazed at the Frenchwoman's memory for detail. "Also my grandmother's."

"Your *grand-mère* had excellent taste. Did you know the moonstone has magical properties? It is the lover's stone, they say."

"What kind of magical properties?" Sara asked, somewhat intrigued, though, she supposed, unless it could magically transform Lord Sharpton into a toad or allow Harry to walk through prison walls, it was little more than a friendly intrigue.

"Some call it superstition, but the stone is only to be given by one's true love," she replied, her lips curling up in a rather mischievous smile. "I had wondered if your betrothed had gifted it to you."

"No," Sara answered, her mind wandering back to that night when she'd escaped Lord Sharpton's first clumsy attempts to be free with her. Lord Sharpton hadn't touched the stone at all. When it fell from her dress, it was Harry who had rescued it. A smile teased at her lips at the memory, before it was chased away by the fact he was now in the village lock-up. She let out the smallest sigh. "He did not."

"I see," the baroness replied, and there was something about the way she said it, with her keen eye and arched brow that made Sara uncomfortable. Perhaps the Frenchwoman did see. "My dear, nothing is ever done until it is truly done. I would not be with my dear husband if my parents had had their way. I would be married to some important French *comte* with bad teeth and a worse temper, but many francs. But my heart and happiness was with a better man. Less power, less money perhaps, but more heart."

The baroness's eyes strayed to her husband, who was in animated conversation with the Duke and Duchess of Weymouth. As if he sensed her, he looked up immediately, and Sara had the sense she had just witnessed a tender, wordless conversation between lovers.

When the last of the guests had departed, Sara turned her mind to Harry. With Lord Sharpton's absence, which promised to last a fortnight, the tension she'd unknowingly held in her shoulders started to ease.

Harry had implored her the night of the ball to tell her father about what had happened, but it had been impossible. The Whitmores did not air their private sins to the world. Appearance was everything. Not only that, but her marriage would save them all from the far greater scandal of retrenchment. Her future was a *fait accompli*, but Harry? She had no idea if he'd ended up in the stocks. Sara had taken Lord Sharpton at his word, but whether she could trust it was debatable. At least when it came to the subject of leniency.

If Harry was going to be kept in the stocks, he was likely being kept in the lock-up in the village. She'd never had cause to visit it before, but she'd seen the small, dreary structure from the road and heard stories about it. Prisoners often had only the most meagre of rations, often paid out of their own pocket, and supplemented by family if they were lucky. Harry had no family that she knew of.

She donned one of her simpler gowns, a butter yellow polonaise, and a *bergère* with a matching ribbon. The wide-brimmed straw hat would protect her from the sun and the curious gazes of onlookers at the lock-up. After a trip to the kitchens where she gathered a small flagon of ale, some cheese, biscuits, and anything else she could scrounge to pack away in a small basket, she headed out, her heart racing in worried anticipation. What state would he be in? Would he even wish to see her? The idea that he might send her away pricked at her, though the reasons why it might be so hurtful were too dear for her to examine closely. And, there was nothing she could do about it, could she? She was betrothed, after all.

Sara had barely gotten past the front park when she'd heard two gardeners speaking in low, hushed voices, catching her attention and slowing her steps.

"They'll probably leave 'im to rot," said one of the under gardeners, his lower lip pursed in disapproval. "Lock-up's full. They 'ad to stow in him the Old Tower."

"Poor bastard," the other shook his head. "Sharpton probably had them throw away the key. Rumor has it Boxford's marked."

The other man's eyes widened, as if he'd just heard a horrible secret. Marked? What did that mean?

Sara had not visited the Old Tower since she was a small child, though it had been one of her favorite places to play. Much of Langdon Park had been modernized by successive viscounts, including her father. Indeed, given the state of her father's finances, he probably should have left what work he'd done for any heirs that she and Lord Sharpton would produce. But the Old Tower—if it had another name it had been lost to history—stood alone, perhaps an old watchtower, or part of a wall or ancient barricade that had fallen away, civilized by gardens and lawn. Her grandmother had indulged her by allowing her to visit, and they, along with her nanny, would have little picnics nearby. It was at a far flung part of the estate, a remnant of an ancient house that had long turned to rubble. It took Sara nearly half an hour to reach it, but after a brisk walk through a series meandering paths and a thick covering of trees, the ancient structure revealed itself.

Sara put a hand to the crown of her bergère, holding it in place as she leaned her head back to study the tower from top to bottom. There was only one entry point inside—a rough and heavy wood door with a large, ancient lock. A small stool, currently unoccupied, suggested a guard was nearby. Cautiously, she climbed the series of crumbling steps leading to it, then pounded on the door. No answer. After several attempts and a rather sore hand, she descended the steps again, circling the tower, looking for any signs of life beyond the birdsong and hum of insects in the warm summer afternoon. Opposite the door, high above her, was a lone window. Was this where they were keeping him?

"Hello!" she called as loudly as she dared.

No response. Placing the basket at her feet, she cupped her hands to her mouth, and projected her voice more forcefully.

"Hello up there!" She paused. "Harry? It's Lady Sara. I brought you some food."

Anxious moments passed, Sara watching for any sign of a returning guard, but the only sound came from the crickets chirping in the grass. She called out a couple of more times without any response. Perhaps the gardeners were wrong, she thought ruefully, and now she had wasted an entire afternoon. She picked up her basket and turned away slowly, taking a few tentative steps before casting one last glance over her shoulder toward the window. A flash of a movement caught her attention, bringing her to a halt. She whirled around.

"Harry?" she called out. "Please come to the window. I'm so sorry for what's happened." And she was terribly sorry. "I didn't mean for this to happen to you. I am sorry you have been treated so shamefully."

A male form appeared in the window, and Sara's heart squeezed. From this distance, it was hard to make out the finer details of his appearance, but it was undoubtedly him. A lock of his hair fell down into his face.

"Are you well?" she asked, his expression inscrutable.

"Yes, my lady."

Sara smiled bitterly at this response. His voice was calm and measured as it almost always was. But she worried how he'd been treated. Given how roughly Lord Sharpton handled her, Sara couldn't imagine that Harry would be spared his wrath.

She smiled, hoping he'd say more. Instead, he walked away from the window.

Sara frowned. "Where are you going?"

Nothing.

"Harry, please," she continued, her voice an undisguised plea. "I'll help you. I promise. I got you into this mess, and I will get you out."

"Yes, my lady."

It was remarkable to Sara that Harry could say something entirely different from the mere inflection of his voice. Because this time, the "yes my lady" sounded remarkably like "I don't believe you." Or, quite possibly, "get stuffed."

"Don't you want my help?" she asked. "I will speak to the guard as soon as he returns and demand he allow me to see you."

While she was being perfectly serious about her intent, Harry's response was a bitter chuckle.

"Yes, my lady."

That one sounded very much like a "no."

Sara put her hands on her hips, her concern now layered with the slightest hint of annoyance.

"Is it 'yes, my lady,' you wish my help, or 'yes, my lady,' I don't?"

Sara stood, waiting for an answer that was, apparently, not coming. The smile she'd tried to keep on her face made her cheeks ache. After a moment of infuriating silence, she threw up her hands and let out a loud, exasperated sigh. Why on earth was he being so singularly obstinate? It wasn't like him.

Or was it?

Sara waited another agonizing moment. She crossed her arms, then paced across the grass, trying to consider her next move, fuelled by a tiny but growing sense of indignation. Over the past weeks—years in fact—her future actions had been dictated first by her father, and soon by Lord Sharpton. She was not about to be vexed by another man. Harry Boxford was going to take her help, whether he wanted it or not. After all, she wasn't going to start her married life wracked with guilt over an assistant gamekeeper. But first she needed to get him to talk to her, and he was clearly in no mood for conversation.

"Are you not hungry at least? Or thirsty?" she called out, then looking to her basket, she groaned. She'd come here with no plan—only good intentions. They were not enough to save him. "I brought food, but when I set out I didn't expect you to be here. I have no way to get it up to you. I don't supposed you have any sort of rope you could let down?"

He remained silent, but even from forty feet below she could see the look of undisguised incredulity in his face.

"Right. That was silly. If you had a rope you would no doubt have used it to escape." Sara paused, waiting for him to say something, but his reply was to move away from the window once again. "I can tell you're brooding, Harry Boxford. And while you are not a lord, at the moment you are acting almost as imperious as one," she continued. "But I am a lady who is quite used to dealing with impervious men."

"A kiss, my lady."

Four words, this time. Not three. She paused, replaying them in her head.

Had Harry Boxford, who rarely said anything at all, just asked for...a kiss?

Sara shouldn't have been distracted by the idea at all. She should have been shocked. Her cheeks were flushed, and it should have been from indignation, or anger. She was to be a married woman, after all. If Lord Sharpton or her father found out, they would forego any second thoughts about leniency and let Harry Boxford rot in the tower for certain. And that was quite the opposite of what she'd come here to accomplish.

Still, the request was not only outrageous...it was tempting.

And a viscount's daughter shouldn't be tempted by kissing an assistant gamekeeper. Even if he did have full lips that commanded her attention. And strong arms to hold her with.

Sara's heart pounded. She looked up at the window and to her surprise, he stood there, an impish grin on his face that made her weaken at the knees ever so slightly.

"Did say you wanted a—" She faltered, embarrassment flushing her cheeks. "A kiss?"

"Yes, my lady."

A curious excitement rose in her chest, leaving her tummy fluttering. And though they were in a nearly forgotten part of the estate with no one around for at least a mile, she realized, to her horror, she was flirting. Flirting with a man to whom she was not intended. Nor ever could be.

Was that why Harry was playing these games with her? To protect her? Or merely remind her of their relative positions in the world?

"Harry Boxford, are you trying to be rid of me?"

"Yes, my lady."

He turned away, disappearing back into the darkness of

the cell above. Retreating into himself where she could not reach him. If there was one sensation she could not abide, it was confinement. It was one she was becoming far too familiar with of late.

Sara waited for a while longer, watching the window for any possible hint that he was nearby. She'd called out a few more times, but received no response. *Stubborn man and his foolish pride.* Since when did Harry show her anything but kindness and companionship that bordered on indulgence?

The question had barely formed in her mind when the answer came rushing in behind it: *When Lord Sharpton tried to assault her and he turned into a fierce protector.*

The sound of rustling brush, perhaps from an animal, or far more likely, a returning guard, caught Sara's attention. She paused, swallowed, then peered into the verge to her left where the sound appeared to be coming from. She'd already lingered here too long. If she was found talking about kissing and keys or even the color of the sky with Harry Boxford, she didn't want to think about the consequences for either of them—Harry especially.

He'd been trying to send her away. Still trying to protect her now, perhaps.

But that was not his duty.

Impatience yielded to frustration, frustration to something else. Something that felt like determination.

She gripped her basket and turned away, her mind churning on a plan.

She was getting Harry out of the Old Tower whether he liked it or not.

CHAPTER 6

*H*arry shuffled on the hard floor, his eyes still closed, barely awake after a restless sleep. His back was wedged up along the space where the wooden floor of the Old Tower met the cold stone of its walls. By comparison, his rough straw mattress and scratchy homespun blanket that counted as his bed in the kennels was almost the stuff of royalty.

A full day and night had passed since Lady Sara had presented herself outside his window, calling up to him. In her yellow dress she'd looked like a buttercup in a field of green—fresh and pretty as always.

But seeing her made him feel…Christ, it made him *feel*. Feel so many things, comforting and frightening in equal measure. She'd come to find him. And, judging from the provisions she'd brought, she'd intended to make sure he knew he wasn't alone. That she worried about him. The action had left him humbled and speechless. And for a terrifying moment, made him wonder if she did actually see him as more than a servant who was, in fact, paid to do her bidding.

That stupid demand of his…for a kiss…what in the hell had he been thinking?

He'd been thinking that even though he was forty feet above, locked behind ancient stone and oak and iron, that she'd wiggled herself right under his skin, and dangerously close to his heart. And he needed to send her away. Especially before that lumbering oaf of a guard found her, and snitched about her presence to Lord Sharpton.

Of course, the rush of blood that rose in her chest and turned her cheeks a shade of pink so bright he could still see the glow from his height…*that* had made him want to scale down the tower and peel the petals off that buttercup and discover what lay at her center.

He shifted as his body, even now, roused at the thought. All the more reason for him to keep her at a safe distance.

The clatter of his chains disrupted his dreams, and he stilled again, aware now of the salty tang of roasted meat tickling his nose.

Was he now dreaming of ham? He'd not eaten much more than a few scraps of hard bread since they tossed him in the tower. Perhaps he was going mad. The last time he'd dreamt of such things was when he was a young lad, going to bed with an empty belly.

Drowsy, he took in a long breath. The smell of the ham was joined by other, equally pleasurable aromas—bread, stewed apples, and…honeysuckle?

His senses jolted him fully awake, and he scurried to his feet—no mean feat with leg irons limiting his movement and throwing him off balance. An old terror found him. Horrible things happened inside prisons. The sun was barely over the horizon, and with only a single, western facing window, it was dark inside save for the warm light of a single lantern.

"You've nothing to fear," came the urgent reply, reassuring and female. "It's me. I brought you something to eat."

Harry dragged his hand over his face and let out a ragged breath, forcing himself into the present. Squinting in the dark, the light from a tin lantern cast a magical glow that stretched along the threads of Lady Sara's fine skirts. Her hands were clasped in front of her, and a long, thick curl of her honey-brown hair draped over one shoulder. It tantalized and confused the hell out of him, all at the same time. Which, if he were in a better place to think about it, explained his feelings for Lady Sara in a nutshell.

"Ham, cheese, some bread, apples, and eggs," she continued brightly, gesturing to a large basket on the floor between them. "And a bit of ale. I hope you like it."

Like it? Harry let out a ragged breath that might have been laughter if he wasn't so damned thirsty. It sounded like a feast. And so was she, with her lush breasts and soft lips turned up in a smile. *She's a lady, for Christ's sake*, Harry admonished himself. But a sight as beautiful as she could make a man forget he hadn't eaten in two days.

And what on earth was a lady doing, delivering it to him? Did Sharpton know she was here, talking to him?

"What are you doing here?" His confusion mixed with fear, leading to a tone that was more abrupt than he intended. Her lashes fluttered in response, like butterfly wings, and it was clear she was taken aback by his response. He cleared his throat, making an effort to take the harshness out of his voice. "This is no place for a lady."

"Well, this is something at least," she said, determined, it seemed, not to be put off by his outburst. "Far better than 'yes, my lady' and 'no, my lady'. This is almost...conversation."

Harry answered her with silence. It hung between them as the sharp, almost painful awareness of need threaded the air. As if responding to it, she walked to him, her jaw taut, her lips pressing together. She laid a hand on his, and it took all of his will not to sink into her.

"I'm sorry," she said, her voice just above a whisper.

Two words, so earnestly spoken. Somewhere deep inside, he could feel part of him soften—that part of him that once, a very long time ago, had someone who'd cared about him. The last time he'd been in prison, no one had come for him. No one had apologized for the series of events that had put him in irons and facing the gallows. But instead of yielding, allowing Lady Sara's earnest caring to wiggle its way into his heart, Harry found himself pushing back against the sensation. *She doesn't really care for you,* he reminded himself. And if she did, she was to marry a blackguard who would no doubt punish her in some fashion for showing Harry mercy.

He shrugged, shrinking from her touch. He couldn't bear her softness now. He had to keep himself focused if he was going to figure out a way to escape.

"How did you get in here?"

"Bribery," she replied. "There are two men outside that door. A quarter hour of your time comes at a stiff price."

She smiled, as if trying to make a bawdy joke, but he was not in a joyful mood. If that bastard Sharpton or Lord Whitmore were keeping such a heavy guard on him, they must have a vested interest in keeping him in…and everyone else out.

"You should go. Your betrothed will be furious with you."

Her hands dropped to her sides, and her chin rose in that way the aristocracy had no doubt been taught from birth to master.

"If he decides to break our betrothal, I believe I could cope quite well with the change in my circumstances. I said I was going to help you, Harry Boxford, and so I am." She crossed her arms, then walked past him. "But the clock is ticking…I have fifteen minutes so let's not waste another minute arguing. You must eat."

He turned at the sound of her rustling skirts. She was

kneeling near the basket, the lantern illuminating her face, and she pulled out a tin plate and began heaping it with food. She presented it to him, with a small flagon of ale and a look of expectation that pierced his skin and went through to his heart.

"You are a lady. You should not be serving me."

"And you should not have interfered that evening between myself and Lord Sharpton," she replied matter of factly, "But here we are."

Humbled, he turned and lowered himself close to her, but not too close. She set the plate near him, the intoxicating smell of sustenance overcoming any sense of polite restraint. He grabbed the plate and tried not to eat like a gut-foundered animal, but the salty meat, fresh bread thick with butter, and stewed apple went down so fast he barely tasted them, followed by a swig of ale he could not swallow as fast as his body demanded. He'd barely set the flagon down before he noticed she was filling his plate again, then presented it to him with a fork and a cloth for his hands. He silently chided himself for his lack of manners, but she only smiled as he accepted the fork, and continued on as if he hadn't just devoured an entire plate of food with his hands.

"I overheard the servants this morning," she said, her voice lowered. "Is it true you are being sent to the assizes?"

So she knew then. He acknowledged her question with the briefest of nods and continued eating. Even in the dim light he could see the blood draining from her cheeks.

"And to think I've been worried about you being in the lock-up or the stocks." She rose to her feet and walked the perimeter of the cell, her keen eye going over every inch, her mouth a hard line. "I will speak to my father today about this entire debacle. And about these conditions. They are intolerable."

Her voice shook a little at the end, and Harry couldn't

decide if it was anger or sadness that had done it, but it touched him as surely as if she'd just reached out to him.

"I doubt his Lordship would be pleased to know that you have inside knowledge of my conditions," he said, and the way her mouth flattened into a tight smile only confirmed his opinion. He took another swallow of ale, wiped his chin, then took a slice of bread to mop up the juices on his plate. "Compared to prison they are quite tolerable, my lady. I do not have to worry about who might attack me in my sleep, nor wish to fight me over a crust of mold-ridden bread."

Her brows dipped, and her lips pursed as she was clearly turning over this new information in her mind. Harry bit back a curse. *Just eat your bloody food, Boxford.* He'd revealed too much. For months they'd been together and he'd barely said two words to her. Now? He couldn't stop flapping his gums.

He ate more slowly now, and while he filled his belly, he consumed himself with assessing every delicate movement of Lady Sara's fingers, every flicker of her brows. Her eyes were fierce and proud and she was attempting nonchalance, but there was a subtle movement in her throat that suggested a hint of nerves. Her pace slowed, and she came to a stop a few feet away. She was at war with herself, perhaps—if she could appear brave, perhaps she could convince herself she was.

"Yesterday, you asked me for a kiss," she said at last.

Harry shook his head, and he could feel the blood creeping into his cheeks.

"That was a mistake, my lady." He'd been angry, tortured by the idea that she had casually given his name to Sharpton for punishment. He'd sought to shock her—to send her away. And he thought it had worked. But now that she was standing here in front him, he wanted nothing more than the chance to taste her.

"Was it?" She paused; bit her bottom lip in a way that was

utterly artless and enthralling all at once. "Because I have given it some thought, and I should like you to kiss me, Harry."

Harry blinked.

She looked away, just for a second, and he could see her bravado fading. Her smile stayed in place, but he suspected it was to convince herself, and not him, that her question was a perfectly acceptable one.

It wasn't, of course. It wasn't acceptable. But it was so damned tempting.

"That is, if you want to," Lady Sara said, her eyes wide, but touched by a hint of trepidation, her hands clasped together at her front. "You asked me yesterday for a kiss. I couldn't grant it. But today, I can. If you wish it."

Was she real, Lady Sara? Because it seemed an angel was before him, or a miraculous fairy, ready to grant him a wish. And he knew he shouldn't. He was beneath her in every possible way. His hands were rough from toil and marked by his crime. And though he would never be accused of vanity, standing in her presence he was keenly aware of his bedraggled appearance; his dirty hands, and the stains on his shirt.

But she wasn't looking at him with disdain. He was keenly aware of her gaze, the intensity of it bringing a rush of heat under his skin. She'd licked her lips, perhaps from sheer nervousness, but the act had, along with her words, signalled an invitation.

His own need overcame reason, overcame the boundaries that society had put on them both. Ignoring the rattle from the chains on his legs, he brought himself to his feet next to her, cupped her face in his hands, and brought his mouth down to hers.

"Yes, my lady."

CHAPTER 7

Sara knew people kissed on the lips, but she'd never witnessed it. Her parents had little affection for each other, and she'd had no other guide for what a kiss should be. Years ago, her grandmother had suggested that a kiss should make one's feet lift from the ground, which Sara had thought was a little fantastical. How on earth could one person make another levitate with a simple touch of the lips? It sounded like magic.

With the right person, her grandmother had said, everything from the smallest touch to the deepest kiss, was magic. Sara's parents had said her grandmother was a silly old woman.

But as there was nothing silly about this. Harry's lips were warm, and a little rough, tasting like the ale he'd just drunk, but not displeasing. She found herself closing her eyes, allowing her to focus solely on his touch, and the glorious sensations that touch elicited in her body. His thumb idly stroked her cheek and if she could bring herself to ponder it at the moment, she would have marvelled at the irony of a man whose hands had been calloused by work, touching her with such tenderness. It was a stark contrast to Lord Sharpton, whose touch ran from polite detachment to predatory and angry with nothing in between.

The mix of sensations—the roughness of his whiskers, the heat of his body next to hers, so masculine and raw, drove away all thoughts of Lord Sharpton and her parents. Harry's mouth began teasing her own, her body rising as a river of heat coursed through her. Gripping the loose folds of his coarse shirt with her fingers, her lips parted for him as he stroked them gently with his tongue. All traces of self-doubt evaporated, and she found herself consumed by the need for so much more. More of him. She kissed him back, mimicking his movements to the point where she thought she heard a groan escape him, and he pulled her body even closer to his.

She breathed the smallest of sighs as her body focused on this new sensation of being stroked and licked and nuzzled by his mouth, back to her ear and—dear heavens—down the side of her neck. Somewhere, in the deeper recesses of her consciousness, she became vaguely aware of her body being lifted right up on her toes. All because of Harry's kiss.

Like magic.

Unlike Lord Sharpton's hands, which were made soft from lack of use, Harry's were strong and hard. And yet, unlike Lord Sharpton, Harry used them only to give her pleasure, running them playfully down the side of her neck, along the ridge of her neckline.

There were a dozen reasons why she'd insisted on finding Harry. Yes, she'd been driven by her own guilt. Yes, to give him some sustenance. Yes, to discover why a man who owed her nothing would come to her aid when those who should have protected her would not. There was something more, though...a need, deep inside of her, that wanted a kiss. And more than that. Tenderness. And she received it.

But it awoke something else in Sara she didn't quite understand. A need for connection. For affection. The grim but firm path of her life had somehow unraveled at his touch, awakening her to something unexpected. Her body wanted him. Her heart wanted him.

He broke the kiss, and another sensation—frustration—created a new kind of urgency in her body. She kept her eyes closed, unwilling for the embrace to end. Instead, she felt his hands on her shoulders and the telltale sounds of metal scraping against the floor as he took a step back.

"You should go," he said softly, clearing his throat. "If your father discovers you were here, it will do neither of us any good. Especially you."

His words settled on her like ice water. Sara opened her eyes, the jumble of pleasurable sensations and unsatisfied longings warring inside with his stark warning.

"Harry," she began, "how can you be concerned about me at a time like this? I overheard the servants in the kitchen this morning. They are sending you to the assizes." The large prisons were a hellish existence and often the only way out was via the gallows or death from disease or malnourishment.

He nodded curtly, swallowing before he answered.

"Yes, my lady." He said it matter-of-factly enough, but despite his efforts, Sara detected a hint of fear. And then, his gaze settled on her. "But I will always be concerned for you."

Sara blinked. How could she deserve his concern? He gave it so selflessly to her. But this was not the time to be distracted by emotion.

"And I will never rest until I can find a way to get you out of here," she replied. She had to save him. Her fate was fixed. His didn't have to be. "You will not rot in prison if I have anything to do about it."

He laughed bitterly. "I won't go to prison, my lady. They wouldn't waste the space on me."

Sara took a step back, a pit opening in her stomach as the implication of Harry's assertion settled on her like a lead cloak.

"Why?" she managed to say, her voice shaking. "Is this because you bear a mark? I heard them speak of it. I don't know what it is."

"It means I did something I should have hanged for."

Sara's eyes widened, before she recovered herself. "People are hanged for many reasons, Harry. Some deserved. Others not. What did you do that marked you for death?"

HARRY LET OUT the smallest breath, then held up his left hand. He'd spent a lifetime trying to mask the T-shaped scar on the pad of his thumb, and revealing it to her felt as though he was showing the ugliest part of his past. She took a step toward him and reached out for his hand, her fingers curling over his own. Harry savoured every touch, and despite the urgency of the moment—or possibly because of it—his body reacted. He fought his own urge to pull her hands to his mouth, to run his fingers over every curve of the body he knew was there, encased in silk and petticoats and pins.

Her fingers traced over the T that had been burnt into his flesh. The scar had faded a little over time, making it easier to hide. He'd learned over the years that some people cared about it and others did not. The Bloody Code had turned many a working man into a criminal.

"I was a poacher. And a good one. Until I was caught. I worked for my uncle. He was a poacher, too—one of the best."

Her eyes flicked up to his face, her head tilted slightly, while her fingers continued to caress his hand. She was just being with him, and though the story was hard to tell, her patient expression made the telling bearable.

"My parents had died, you see. My father was a blacksmith—a good man, an honest, hardworking man. On her deathbed, my mother made my uncle promise to keep me, and he took me in. I suppose if the man had one shred of decency, it was that he kept his word to her.

"I was naught ten years old. Wiry and slight—and quite good at keeping quiet. My uncle saw an opportunity for me to be a lookout for the gamekeepers, and to distract them if necessary while my uncle and his band plied their trade. My uncle was a demanding master. He managed me and his men with his fists, if necessary. "

Harry Boxford, you worthless cur. His uncle's harsh words rang in his ears, and the feeling of the switch on his back could make him flinch even now. *You will earn your keep with me or you will never be back under my roof again.*

He shook off the memory and continued. "When I was thirteen, I gained enough experience to start poaching myself. I was good at it. I knew how to bait the animals in such a way. I was good at my trade, but alas, not good enough. I, and several of my uncle's men were caught. We were held in Marshalsea for months. My uncle left me there. I knew he never thought well of me, but I was still a lad."

She reached out, running trembling fingers along his hairline, her mouth tight, as if she was trying to stifle the anguish that seeped through Harry's skin as he told this story for the first time. Harry swallowed deeply, struggling to keep his emotions in check. Her lips turned up slightly then, in a sad but encouraging smile, drawing the words out of him as if she was drawing poison from a wound.

"I was tried. Poaching is a hanging offence, and several of the men were led to the gallows that day. Indeed, I was supposed to be among them. At the last moment, they pulled me aside, and an older bloke took my place. Said he was done livin' and I still had plenty to do. I watched him hang." He paused then, let go a ragged breath as Jones's voice and twitching feet invaded his thoughts. He'd carefully locked away that hateful memory, and until this moment, he'd never shared it with anyone.

"They let me go," he continued after a painful pause, "but a marked man will only escape the gallows once. If Sharpton brings me before a judge, this will seal my fate." He looked up at her, waiting for the pity, or the disdain, or whatever judgment he'd prepared himself for. Instead, she looked at him with a mix of indignation and determination.

"No, it won't." She brushed a tear from his cheek that he didn't even realize had fallen, her voice clear and purposeful. "Because I am going to help you escape."

A series of loud bangs, like the pounding of a fist from the other side of the door, made both of them start. Clearly, her fifteen minutes were coming to an end.

"No, my lady," he replied, backing away from her. He would not allow her to put herself in harm's way for him. "I'll manage on my own."

"How? You have no weapons."

"I have this," he said, pointing to his temple. He'd spent the past two days watching the guards. During the day there appeared to be two, but three times a day, for short periods, there was only one, as they singularly went off to eat or relieve themselves. "I will have to be transported. Guards can be bribed. Overcome. I can fight. I'm not going to throw my life away. But I will do it alone."

"So you are prepared to throw your life away," Lady Sara responded. "There is one key, and it's on the body of a rather grim, broad man with hands so large I'm certain he could crush you with them if he chose. You haven't eaten in two days. You have heavy shackles, and little money, if any, to bribe anyone. I am not in the habit of thinking of escape plans, but as of this moment you don't have a hope of one, regardless of how quick your brain or your body may be. You need my help, Harry Boxford. And I'm going to give it to you, whether you like it or not."

"My lady, your time is up," came the mumbled warning from the other side of the door. "Time to go."

"One moment," she cried out, before turning to him. "I will be back. I promise."

"Why do you wish to help me?" he asked.

She walked to the door, and turned back to him one last time.

"For the same reason you helped me, Harry."

She disappeared on the other side of the door, and Harry stood there, feet rooted to the ground, almost afraid to breathe.

It couldn't be the same reason. He'd helped her because, goddamn it, he'd fallen in love with her. Ladies did not fall in love with assistant gamekeepers. With men marked for death and holes in their boots.

It was impossible.

CHAPTER 8

The house was still quiet when Sara returned, allowing her to turn her mind to Harry's escape. She was not, by nature, the scheming sort, but she began to churn out the most outrageous of plans, each one more complicated and convoluted than the next. She had nearly a fortnight until Lord Sharpton's return. Surely in that time she would be able to find some means to help him.

Sara started in the library, scouring the shelves for books that might provide guidance for sleeping draughts for overbearing guards, or how to pick locks. But the volumes on her father's shelves were on far less scandalous subjects. When that proved unsuccessful, she wandered to the kitchens, where she spoke to Mrs. Farley, Langdon Park's cook, who complained in hushed tones about the half dozen men of Lord Sharpton's coterie that she was now obligated to feed.

"Three more arrived but an hour ago," the woman grumbled. She was obviously distressed, from the way she took out her frustrations on the potatoes and parsnips she was chopping with more vigor than was required. "Louts, each one. Snoopin' around and carrying on as if they were the masters, and not his Lordship."

Sara only nodded, trying not to give too much away. She'd met two of them this morning—mean looking fellows who'd only acceded to her wishes to visit the tower after she'd dropped a few coins into their hands. Sara reminded Mrs. Farley that when Lord Sharpton married Sara, the unentailed estate would become effectively his after the death of her father—and Lord Sharpton's "louts" would be a part of the household.

The image of Lord Sharpton's men guarding the Old Tower turned Sara's mind to another puzzle: locks. Specifically, the ones on the doors and the padlocks on Harry's shackles. Even if he could overcome the guards, which seemed unlikely, it would be impossible for him to run or safely get down the winding staircase without breaking his neck. She needed a key for those locks—or a way for him to pick them.

Keys in the household were under the watchful protection of the housekeeper, who guarded her chatelaine with a jealous zeal. Even if Sara could concoct a story about losing a key to a jewelry box, there would be no way the housekeeper would "loan" a key, even for a short period of time. Perhaps Mr. Barton—

"Excuse me, Lady Sara."

The rushed voice of an upstairs maid interrupted Sara's pondering, pulling her back into the present.

"Yes?"

"His Lordship is asking that you come to his study directly."

Sara groaned to herself, then obeyed, assuming wedding business was to be the topic of conversation. Her marriage to Lord Sharpton had the singular effect of increasing her parents' interest in her, though it was less about asking her opinions and more about informing her about their decisions.

"Father," she said, entering the study and standing, as she'd long been accustomed to, opposite the massive oak desk. While her parents had often taken delight by exchanging sordid stories about the failings of one family or another, and congratulating themselves for their success in keeping the taint of scandal at bay, the hypocrisy of those tales was never more in evidence than in her father's study. To economize in the least egregious means possible, her father had sold pieces of furniture, rugs, jewelry, and a few rare parcels of land. They'd closed off rooms, and laid off staff. But her father's study, she could not help but notice, had been singular in that not a single item had been pilfered to pay his gaming debts. Not one of the many crystal decanters, the painting by one of the Dutch masters, or the expertly tied Persian rug under her feet had been sold.

"There you are," he said, idly toying with the chain on his quizzing glass before sitting down. "I have good news. Word has just come to me that Lord Sharpton shall be returning no later than Wednesday, and with a very special wedding present for you."

Her father's news rattled Sara, temporarily robbing her of speech. Today was Monday. She put a hand to her chest and prayed that whatever emotion she betrayed—for even now the rush of panic heated her blood—would be construed as excitement instead of alarm.

"That is very generous of him," she said at last, feigning a smile that seemed to placate her father, who appraised her every movement. In truth, she neither wished or nor cared for a wedding present from Lord Sharpton. Like every other daughter of the peerage, her marriage was contractual, not romantic. Love matches were for fairy tales. There was only one thing she desired, and that was Harry.

Stop. You can't desire Harry. You can only desire his escape.

"Generous indeed," he continued. "It seems he has done you the honor of obtaining a special license."

Sara faltered and her stomach lurched, but she managed to pause long enough to acknowledge her father. Dear heavens...was that her wedding present? "That is excellent news," she managed to say, "though hardly necessary."

"Lord Sharpton is not the type of man who leaves anything to chance. When he wants something, he pursues it," he replied. "This is a great compliment to you. And, to be certain, saves this family a great expense."

Sara fought the prick of tears at the back of her eyes as her stomach lurched. At that moment, she feared she would be sick over her father's Persian carpets. She reached out a shaky hand to a nearby settee, and lowered herself with as much grace as her body would allow.

Her father's eyes narrowed. "Are you not pleased?"

"I am..." Sara groped for words amidst the fog that had clouded her brain. She could be married by Wednesday, if arrangements had already been made. "It seems very quick, Father. Are you in such a rush to be rid of me?"

Her question genuinely seemed to take her father aback.

"Of course not. But you are a woman now. You should have had a season last year, but circumstances forbade it."

Circumstance stances being her father's gaming debts, no doubt, but she did not see fit to argue.

"Being married by special licence is a highly exclusive event," he continued, animated, and Sara realized he was trying to placate her to some small degree. "To be seen as sought after in such a particular fashion by such a powerful man as Viscount Sharpton will bode very well for the family. And save us much expense," he repeated.

Right. In the end it came to that. Saving money and saving face. She sat even straighter in her chair, if such a thing were possible, buoyed by a glimmer of inspiration. She wanted to save something too. Or, someone.

"Would it be unseemly to ask for a wedding present? One that would be of no cost to you."

She wasn't sure if it was the question, or the condition on the question that captured her father's attention, but he nodded slightly, acknowledging her request. This was her moment, and she needed to take it. She drew in a quick breath.

"I desire a pardon for Harry Boxford."

Her father waved away her request as if he was swatting a fly. "I do not see why you should have so much interest in the life of an assistant gamekeeper, of all things. It does not do for a Whitmore to concern themselves in the lives of those beneath them."

She wished to correct him then—tell him that of all the people in her life, Harry was the only one who'd shown her the slightest bit of concern. But that would derail her request entirely, so she took another approach.

"I was told he would merely be locked in the stocks, but this is not the case," she said. "I was given Lord Sharpton's word."

"Lord Sharpton made it quite clear that the prisoner is his responsibility, and I shall not interfere," he replied, his voice suddenly hard and low, putting Sara on her guard. When her father spoke in whispers, it never bode well. Whitmores were never loud, lest the servants were at the door—but the clipped tones and harsh edges on every other syllable, coupled with cheeks as scarlet as the heels of his shoes, betrayed his anger. "What in the blazes were you doing at the Old Tower this morning?"

Sara clasped her hands firmly in her lap as her father started fiddling with his quizzing glass again, pacing the floor. She swallowed, daring to look him in the eye, wondering who'd alerted him to her early morning escapade to see Harry. Harry's warning echoed in her memory.

They are watching.

She hadn't taken Harry very seriously then. She'd thought he was being melodramatic, which was utterly ridiculous, given Harry's generally practical nature. They'd been friends, she'd told herself. His company had been purely benign, a circumstance born of proximity. Everyone knew she was destined for a man of title and fortune—that had been her fate since birth. What did it matter if she'd wandered to the kennels to visit the puppies, or went for a stroll on the lawn because she couldn't sleep and happen to meet him as he walked by? All she'd wanted was a bit of freedom before the inevitable walls of marriage trapped her inside. It couldn't have meant anything. But she was wrong.

Apparently, it meant everything. Including Harry's life.

"Father, Harry Boxford's service to this estate has been very valuable, and I wanted to see to his situation. I found him shackled and without food or water for nearly two days," she replied, attempting to keep her tone dispassionate even as her insides coiled with anger. "Father you must—"

"I cannot fathom why you are so enraptured with this man's wellbeing."

Her father's eyes narrowed, and Sara realized she was veering into dangerous territory. His gaze washed over her, lingering for but a moment on her belly before resting on her face. The implication was not lost on Sara. If, for any reason either her father or Lord Sharpton suspected anything untoward between them, Harry Boxford was a dead man. And when she considered the circumstances she'd found him in, she couldn't help but wonder if that was Lord Sharpton's goal, one way or another.

She straightened, allowing the insinuation to pass over her, careful not to feed her father's passing suspicions.

"Because he has been a loyal servant on this estate," she replied earnestly. "As I would do for Mrs. Farley, Mr. Barton, or any of the others."

"Take care to remember with whom your wellbeing lies, daughter. I will not toss away our security because of your missish concerns for the plight of the riff raff," he spat, the vehemence causing his nostrils to flare and his voice to shake. "Do not further tax the air with his name. You will be married before the week is done. Make yourself ready."

He turned away from her and went to the window, clasping his hands behind him to signal her dismissal. She rose, walked to the door, then tore off to her bedchamber. Adding insult to injury, when she arrived there were two ladies' maids to greet her, the women going through Sara's pulling out panniers and gowns and corsets. Her mother had sent them, they said, to prepare her wardrobe for Lord Sharpton's return. Claiming a headache, she dismissed them, allowing herself a few moments of self-pity as her gaze trailed out the windows. Somewhere past the treeline was the Old Tower. She opened the window, allowing a rush of fresh air to clear her head as she sharpened her mind.

Shackles, but no key. A forty foot tower, with one guarded door. And one day to help Harry escape.

CHAPTER 9

*H*arry leaned against the stone window frame of the tower and watched billowing clouds float lazily across the summer sky, carried along by a stiff afternoon breeze. Even though they appeared free, the clouds were subject to invisible, greater forces that directed their movement, just like him. Even Lady Sara, in her privileged position, was not immune.

Yesterday's kiss had been ill advised. A man didn't make his point about not wishing to be alone by immersing himself in the sweet, merciful embrace of a woman. But most surprising of all was that she'd welcomed his touch—asked for his touch—even though his hands were rough and he wasn't nicely groomed or perfumed. She was so soft, and her body had melted as he'd run his lips over the soft peaks and valleys of her face, neck and shoulders.

It had scared the hell out of him how much he needed her. How much he missed her now.

How could he miss something he was never supposed to have? Everything about her was forbidden. Even if she wasn't a lady—even if she wasn't supposed to be another man's wife —Harry had long ago decided that he was better off alone. But right now he would have sold every ounce of his soul just to spend another moment with her.

Was it pity, he wondered, that had brought her here? Or to assuage her own conscience? Or, dare he think it, something else?

It had to be her conscience, Harry reasoned. She'd become fixated on helping him escape, which was ironic, given the fact she was trapped herself.

It had been Harry's choice to deal with Sharpton. To pull that shameless bastard off her and punish him for the way he'd treated someone so precious. Someone who, if circumstances were different, might have been his.

And when he had those treacherous thoughts, he packed them up and buried them safely away, until they reared themselves again. He didn't even know when they had begun. Slowly, no doubt, unfolding over days and weeks and months, tucking into the corners of his consciousness when he wasn't paying attention.

Every time she came to the kennels to pet the dogs, she stayed, just for a few minutes at a time. And in those small visits she let slip smallest pieces of her world that gave Harry insights into this remarkable and lonely girl who liked to sew and hated to paint, who liked dogs but was entirely uncertain about cats. She talked about her grandmother, who raised her and was rumoured to have the blood of Travellers; a fact which was not to be spoken of in polite company but, she admitted in hushed, exasperated tones, was probably the most interesting thing about her.

And somewhere in the midst of mostly one-sided conversations about stitching and cats, Travellers and family secrets, Harry had slowly, impossibly, gone and fallen in love with her.

"Harry?"

The sound of his name drew his attention from the clouds back down to earth. Forty feet below she stood in skirts that were truly voluminous. Her lips were pulled into a tight smile, and there was something uneasy in her expression that made his hackles rise.

"I have been given leave to bring you fresh provisions," she called up, her voice politely detached. "Please ensure you are presentable."

Harry wanted to smile. Instead, he nodded curtly. He knew the two accompanying her, and while he considered them of a decent sort, he wasn't certain if they were under her father's or Sharpton's thumb.

He walked away from the window, anticipation coiling in his body. He heard the heavy jangling of keys in the lock, the sound of footsteps on the stone steps that snaked up one side of the tower, and at last, the scraping of the bolt immediately on the other side of the door.

"Good afternoon," she said primly, in the way her class had of addressing staff, before turning to the guard standing behind her. "You will wait outside. I shall call when I am ready."

"You've five minutes," the guard croaked.

"I will have ten, or my father shall hear of it," she replied.

"I don't answer to him, my lady," he replied gruffly.

Harry remained still, though inside he wanted to choke the impertinence right out of the hopper-arsed guard. But as good as Harry could be in a fight, he'd wouldn't stand a chance against an armed man who could call on two more if needed, especially with Lady Sara getting in the middle.

The door closed behind her with a heavy groan. At the thumping sound of the footsteps going back down the tower, her shoulders slumped and her face fell into a worried frown.

"Lord Sharpton is due to arrive by noon tomorrow," she said in a hurried, hushed whisper. "You must get away before he does."

She reached into her skirt, obviously fishing something out of her pocket, then pulled out a key.

"Where did you get that?"

"Mr. Barton." She pressed it into his hands.

"He gave you one of his master keys?"

"Not exactly," she said, wearing a sheepish grin. "I went to speak to him about the hunting dogs…breeding a special one for Lord Sharpton. While he was distracted, I nicked it."

Harry put the key in the padlock that held the shackles at his feet. It opened with a satisfying click.

"It won't get you on the other side of the door," she continued, "but once you are out you'll at least be able to run."

"I'll definitely have a fighting chance," he continued.

"There are now three men on the other side of the door." She frowned. "So you'll need something else."

Lady Sara began hitching up her skirts, petticoats and all, which stunned Harry into silence. Two shapely legs were revealed; white silk stockings hugging the curves of her calves, and delicate garters at her knees. Framing her was a wide cage that exaggerated her hips to the point where her elbows could rest upon them. Harry never understood the ridiculous fashion, but now, as he somehow managed to drag his attention away from her calves and delicate ankles, he understood why she wore wearing such a costume. A long length of cord was woven through it, and the entire thing resembled a woven basket.

"I knew he was going to check any chests or baskets I brought, so I had to be more inventive." Completely oblivious to his discomfort, she looked up at him, triumph brightening her already pretty face. "If you can hold up my skirts, I can uncoil it. I knew there had to be something worthwhile about wearing these horrible panniers."

Harry put his hands on his hips, wondering if the gods were playing some sort of cruel joke on him.

"Are you mad?" he said, gesturing toward the rope all the while trying to avoid staring at her legs. "If you are discovered, they are going to use that to hang me on the spot. And heaven knows what would happen to you."

"I know what is about to happen to me," she said, the smile fading from her face. "But you? You can be free."

Harry ran his gaze over her. He would never be free. Not while he knew she was in the hands of that ruffian she'd been condemned to marry.

"These aren't fit to touch such fine silk." He held up his hands. "I'll soil your dress."

A sad smile teased her mouth, and she reached out, brushing her fingers of her right hand along his forearm, then took his hands in hers.

"These are the worthiest hands in the kingdom, Harry Boxford."

Harry swallowed back the rising ache that had grown in his chest. She was looking at him that way again. Like he meant something to the world. Maybe even like he meant something to her.

He pushed the ache away, back into its proper place.

"But you can't bend over in all that boning. You can barely lift your arms." Harry lowered himself to his knees in front of her. In any other time and place, he would think of a million wonderful things he would do to her body, kneeling in front of her like this. But not now. "It will be faster if I unravel it."

She nodded, and with a swish of fabric, she gathered up the layers of silk. Harry forced himself to focus on the task of unwinding the long cable of rope that she'd managed to artfully weave into her skirts and secure at her waist. Before long, it was laid out in a tidy coil at his feet.

"That's better," she said, dropping her skirts, then pointing a series of iron loops in the wall. "You should be able to anchor it there. It is sturdy rope. It will have no problem holding your weight. But you do need to be careful. Do you know how to climb? You seem to know how to do every-thing else."

Everything but keep himself out of a date with a hang-man, he thought, examining the rope. It was sturdy enough. If he used some cloth from his shirt to bind his hands, and left under the cover of night... He would have a better chance than what he had without her help—which was almost none.

"Why are you doing this?" he asked, his heart racing. "Do you have any idea of the risks you are taking? You've seen Sharpton's wrath. They will know you've helped me."

"I am prepared to live with that," she said. "And besides, I thought we were friends."

Harry started at the word. He didn't have friends, and he'd preferred it that way.

"Ladies are not friends with assistant gamekeepers, my lady," he said. "That is not how the world works."

She looked almost wounded then. "Do not claim worldli-ness, Harry. I am about to be married to a man because my parents wish it. I don't love him. I know he doesn't love me. But it doesn't matter, does it? Because it's how the world works. I must marry him. I do not have a choice in this."

Harry raked a hand through his hair, irritation seeping into him. While he did not for a moment think Lady Sara had the same privileges as the men in her sphere, her deter-mination to bend to those who clearly did not have her best interests at heart devastated him. It was bad enough he had this damnable need to see her happy. It was torture to know that the people in her life who could help her to be so, would not.

"Why is that, my lady?" he asked.

"I just told you, Harry," she replied, clearly exasperated. "Women must marry."

"You will excuse me then, because I am a simple man, not privileged to education, so perhaps I am confused. Unenlightened in the ways of my betters," he said, trying without much success to keep the annoyance out of his voice. "Mr. Barton told me the estate is not entailed. There must be only a small handful of women in your position with a fortune of their own, not obligated to marry. Why not use it to your advantage?"

She blinked, as if caught completely off guard. He wanted to shake her, tell her she was worth more than she believed, and my God, that if he could have been worthy to love her, he would. Because he loved her.

"Because that is not how things are done in my family, Harry," she replied. "My parents would consider it an utter scandal if I did not marry. And the Whitmores avoid scandal at all cost."

"The cost being your future," he said bitterly. "Your happiness."

"My happiness is not what is at issue. Women of my class do not marry for happiness. Even if I inherit the estate, it is already mired in considerable debt. Lord Sharpton is a very wealthy man with considerable influence. When he takes possession of Langdon Park...I am certain it will be for the better."

"Sharpton is not fit to take possession of the dirt beneath your feet, my lady. He's not worthy of you."

But I am, he wanted to shout. *I am.* Even though he had

barely two shillings to rub together. Even though he had nothing to offer her but himself.

"What do you want me to do, Harry?" she asked, exasperated. "It's not as if I can marry you."

The words had barely fallen from her lips before Sara wished she could take them back.

"Harry—" she faltered, reaching out to him, but he'd already stepped away, his stone-like expression unable to mask the wound she'd caused. "I didn't mean it that way."

It was impossible for her to be with him. And the reasons were obvious to both of them. Except, until that moment, she'd never given voice to that horrible truth. She couldn't marry him.

"No, my lady, you can't marry me," Harry replied. "But with respect, I don't recall asking. Just as I don't recall asking you for your help. Or your friendship."

Sara started at the harshness of his reply.

"And I didn't ask for you to save me," she replied, tears pricking the backs of her eyes. "But you were so hell bent on being a hero—"

"Ask any of the men in the lock-up I've kept from stealing things that didn't belong to 'em. They'd have some fine words to say about me, and none fit for your ears," Harry said.

"Knocking a drunken man on his arse doesn't make me a hero."

"It made you mine," she said, her throat tightening with emotion she was desperate to keep in check. "Harry, I have to do this. My marriage will save Langdon Park and my family's honor. That has to be worth something."

"Do you see this?" He held out his hand, palm up, displaying red branded mark on the pad of his thumb. "It hurt like hell when they did this to me, and I was happy for it. And not just because I was alive. It was a reminder to me of what happens when you give yourself to a man who will take whatever he can for himself, until you have nothing left of value. And then he tosses you aside, despite all the pretty promises he made to keep you safe. You will be used until you become a liability, until he tires of you, and then he will not care if you live or die. And you'll wish you'd been alone because then the only person who can let you down is yourself."

Sara opened her mouth, but there was nothing she could think to say. Deep down, part of her knew what he said was true. But whether or not Harry was the best man she knew, whether or not his amber eyes warmed her soul, whether or not his quiet ways were welcoming, she had an obligation to her family to do the right thing. It was what was expected of her. She'd known her destiny—and her parents were helping her complete it, all the while being able to save the family from ruin. Maybe she could be her own hero.

A heavy fist banging on the door broke the silence that hung in the air. Sara jumped, then dabbed the corners of her eyes.

"I will come back at nightfall with provisions and—"

He turned away.

"No, my lady."

Sara's heart lurched at Harry's dismissal of her help. Of

her care. From behind, the door scraped open. Wordlessly she turned around and walked away, allowing one of the footmen to assist her down the stairs. Above, the low rumble from the prison door shutting behind them echoed against the stone walls. She climbed into the small cart, determined not to look over her shoulder toward the tower window. Her future was ahead of her—toward Langdon Park, where, one day, she would be mistress of a house that had never truly given her comfort. That had never felt as though it was home.

When she became mistress of Langdon Park, she would have the Old Tower torn to pieces.

Somehow, Sara managed to carry on with the rest of her day without succumbing to the darkness that filled her. On her return, she attempted to put a sense of purpose into her restlessness, walking the endless rooms and galleries, taking mental note of every crack that needed filling in the darker corners of the house, every room that had been nearly emptied of furniture that had been sold to pay her father's debts. She paused at a window in one of countless parlours that had been shuttered, running her finger across a window ledge, her fingertip making a track in a layer of dust. Through an open door that led to an adjoining room, she heard two servants enter, talking amongst themselves in hushed tones.

"The new master will be 'ere tomorrow."

"He's not the master yet," the other servant replied, clearly not approving. Sara recognized the voice of Mrs. Farley.

"Might as well be. As soon as he's married the Lady Sara, the Viscount and Viscountess will be keeping to their house in town."

"I don't see how that could be a good thing," Mrs. Farley replied, letting go a 'tsk-tsk'. "Too many gaming tables in town. That's how his Lordship lost Langdon Park in the first place."

Sara froze. *Lost Langdon Park?*

"I feel sorry for Lady Sara, that's for certain. Having to marry an ogre like Sharpton just to save face for her father's missteps." Mrs. Farley sighed. "Marching a lamb off to the sacrifice. I can barely think on it."

If her stomach wasn't empty, Sara was certain she would have been sick. She stood, fixed to the floor, unable to move as the weight of what she'd heard landed on her shoulders.

This had to be a mistake. Her father had lost the estate? It didn't make any sense.

Sara tore out of the room and ran for her father's study, where he spent most of his afternoons.

"Father, I need to speak with you at once," she said, clearing her throat, her heart pounding.

Her father, as usual, looked slightly perturbed at his daughter's presence. "Sara, whatever is the matter? Has Lord Sharpton arrived early?"

She shook her head. "Are you and mama leaving for London after the wedding?"

His thin eyebrows flattened to a line. "We are. How did you—"

"Is it because you are no longer the owner of Langdon Park?"

"Sara, I need to know the meaning of these questions."

"Why am I being forced to marry Lord Sharpton? If you have lost the estate to him, why must I marry him?"

He looked away from her for a moment, his mouth pursing in thought. When he raised his gaze to her, his voice was brittle.

"Because you were part of the bargain, my dear. I couldn't just lose the estate without having a plan. I can be a fool, but I am not that much of a fool. I am a Whitmore, after all."

Sara wanted to reach out and grasp one of the chairs to steady herself, but was determined not to give her father the satisfaction of seeing her weakness. Instead, she put a hand to her stomach, which rolled as the implication of her father's words took hold.

"You bet..." Sara's voice trailed off as she struggled to gain control of her voice. "You bet my hand—and lost?"

For just a moment, her father appeared contrite.

"Lord Sharpton had all the luck of the cards that day," he said. "The deed to Langdon was all I had left. And I was certain fortune would turn in my favor. But in case it did not, there was the stipulation marriage would be part of the deed."

Sara could barely believe what she was hearing. "But...the family name. The scandal."

"That is the beauty of it, you see?" Her father cleaned his quizzing glass and slid it into his pocket. "No one except you and Sharpton will know. He will take possession, and marriage to you will ensure that society will be none the wiser. All will assume that the inheritance will go as planned. Your mother and I will retire to Whitmore House in London where there will be no whispers about retrenchment."

No wonder her father was so pleased about the special license. The faster his scandal was hidden from the world, the better.

"You...for years have been telling me to behave, to honor the family name, and yet, you act dishonorably." Her voice rose then, choked by tears, but Sara cared not who heard them. "I cannot wait to rid myself of the name of Whitmore. You disgust me."

Unable to bear the sight of her father any longer, Sara ran to her room, locked the door behind her, and sank on to her bed, cursing her own blind stupidity. Harry had tried to tell her that something about this entire affair was wrong, but she wouldn't listen. Because she had been too foolish to see the truth. About Lord Sharpton. About her father.

And mostly, about herself.

She unpinned her dress and, with some difficulty, shed the layers of her fine pink gown and tossed it aside. It was the same gown she'd worn the night of her engagement to Lord Sharpton. She would tear it to pieces before being forced to wear it again. She idly picked through the few pieces of jewelry on her dressing table, and there sat the brooch her grandmother had given her. The Falling Star. It would be given to her by her true love, she'd told Sara. A man worthy of her.

It had been Harry who'd rescued it. Picked it off the ground, and put it into her hands.

A worthy man. A man worth her love.

And soon he'd be leaving her.

She had to find him. This time, she had to save herself. Be her own hero.

Digging in her wardrobe, past fine linen and silks, she found her simplest frock and some sturdy boots. She left her hair in a simple plait, then reached under her bed. She'd packed a very small satchel with a few essentials for Harry, intending to leave them for his escape: a clean shirt, a few coins, and a small handkerchief she'd embroidered with his initials that she'd meant to give to him as a birthday present. Bundling up an extra chemise for herself she went to her jewelry chest and picked out two or three pieces—things she could sell, and the Fallen Star, which would be hers—and tucked them in a small wooden box. She looked into the satchel, uncertain, when one more thought struck her. She dug out her grandmother's shoes—the ones she'd worn the night of her engagement—and carefully wrapped them in the clean chemise. She would not leave them to be sold.

She claimed a headache and sent the servants away when

they came to call her for dinner, and then waited for dusk. Using an old servant's staircase, she crept out of the house and ran for the tower. A heavy cloud had settled overhead. She half walked, half ran, a lantern in her hands.

As the canopy of trees grew thicker, darkness closed in, and Sara had to fight for the ability to stay calm and measured. The path narrowed, and for a moment she hesitated. A light but steady rain had begun to fall, drops finding the ground even through the heavy verdant cover overhead, an insistent rhythm her heart rose to meet.

Would he turn her away? The hurt in his amber eyes had haunted her from the moment she'd caused it. Because Harry loved her, and she'd just told him that, despite everything, he wasn't enough.

But he was everything to her. And Sara wanted everything.

She broke off at a run, a task not easy given the weight of her skirts and heavy oil cloak. Her boots squelched underfoot. In moments, she'd broken through the forest to be confronted by the Old Tower, its grim, dark stone made even more menacing by stone-gray sky.

Her gaze flew immediately to the entry, where Sharpton's man kept watch, but there was no one to be seen. She blew out a breath in relief. Something had to go right for them.

She continued to the west side of the tower, and putting a hand to her brow to shield her eyes from the rain, peered to the top. The rain had slowed, but with the sky still behind a thick layer of cloud, it was becoming difficult to see. There was no sign of him in the window. She cupped her hands to the side of her mouth.

"Harry!"

She stopped and took care to look around again. Aside from the patter of rain on leaves, she seemed to be alone. She turned back to the tower and repeated the gesture, this time forcing her voice a little louder.

"Harry!"

Nothing.

She was walking closer to the Old Tower when the flash of something moving in the breeze caught her eye. She squinted in the darkness, taking a moment for her brain to piece together what she was seeing.

A long line of rope swung aimlessly just above her head.

He'd gone.

Tears stung her eyes, and she wiped them away with the back of her hand, which was cold from the rain. She should not have felt betrayed. He was not supposed to mean anything to her. She was supposed to save him. And maybe she had.

So why did she feel so horribly sad?

It had been a traitorous thought, wanting Harry for her own. Was this why she was crying? Because somewhere, in the deep recesses of her heart, this is what she wanted.

Perhaps being at Harry's side was no place for a lady.

But it would have been the perfect place for Sara.

CHAPTER 11

When Harry's feet had hit the ground at the foot of the Old Tower last night, he'd started running and didn't stop until he'd gone past the boundaries of Langdon Park, past the borders of the nearby village, and waded across a small stream. By the time he'd reached the trees on the other side, perhaps ten miles from the tower, his legs finally gave out. He collapsed on the other side, gulping air, blood pounding in his ears.

He laid there for some time, his eyes closed. It was still the dead of night, and all he had to show for himself was the clothes on his back and the boots on his feet that were worn through. He was utterly alone, and despite any physical discomfort he might have felt, the solitude should have suited him just fine. Just has it always had.

But somewhere past the exhaustion and hunger, there was a void he couldn't recall having before. An unsatisfied yearning as deep and black as any mine.

Lady Sara Whitmore had helped free his body from that tower, but she'd captured his heart and soul.

When he'd crawled down the rope, he had a momentary

urge to go back to the house. But what could he promise her? He'd had nothing to his name but the clothes on his back, and even they were in poor shape. Sneaking out to find her at her balcony, throwing pebbles at her window and hoping she'd call his name was a fool's errand. He'd seen that story once, performed by players at a country fair, and it hadn't worked out particularly well for anyone. Besides, she'd been determined to marry Sharpton.

You know very well I can't marry you.

He'd known that was the truth, but until she'd voiced it, there had been a part of him that dreamt it might be otherwise.

The night wore on, and though his body was desperately tired, the war between his head and his heart deprived him of a good night's rest. He woke before dawn, his weak stomach signalling its protest. First, he'd find a way to hunt for his breakfast. What the hell he was going to do after that, he had no idea.

He sat up, conscious of the way he held himself, conscious of every sound—the scurrying of small animals and the gentle flow of water nearby were the backdrop to an otherwise still morning. The dim twilight of dawn was to his right. He'd go south, toward Staffordshire. It was easier to disappear in the larger towns, and he could find enough work as a laborer to keep his stomach full. He'd briefly toyed with the idea of going back and finding his uncle. His uncle could still be alive, for all Harry knew. Still earning a rough but tidy existence stealing game.

As a boy, Harry had sworn on his father's unmarked grave in an Essex churchyard to be a good, honorable man. But desperation was a fierce master, and fear its whip. It made people do things they shouldn't. Like marrying a bastard of a man to save one's family from public scandal.

God, he wanted to rescue her. But it would be pointless if

she didn't want to rescue herself. If only he could have given her the strength to believe she could choose a different path for herself.

Sunlight streamed through the trees, its warmth finding him at last. Travelling in unfamiliar woods was ill advised at any time, but nights were especially dangerous. He'd been lucky not to have his leg caught in some stray trap. His efforts as Langdon Park's watcher had, for the most part, kept poachers at bay there, but this land was well beyond its borders. He would follow the stream for a time, hoping it led him to a farmer's field or the next village. His absence would be noticed soon, and it was likely Sharpton would send out his men in pursuit.

But first he needed to eat. And to do that, he needed to hunt. Amongst the basket of food she'd provided, Lady Sara had left him a small knife. Its steel blade was sharp and while it might have been helpful once he caught an animal, it would be of little use in catching one. He needed another weapon for that.

He got to his feet and surveyed the ground. By the edge of the stream he found three stones of a good size and shape. Pulling the laces—or what was left of them—from his boots, he fashioned himself a bolas. It was the first weapon he'd ever made for himself—perfect for hunting small game, and if he had few points of pride, one was his ability to expertly take down prey with it.

Oak and ash trees soared overhead, and the forest floor was covered with a mix of fern and old decayed wood. It was a perfect spot for traps, their wide iron jaws tucked beneath the verge. They were his uncle's favorite tool of choice, and Harry suspected it had something to do with the cruelty of the method. As a boy he'd seen an animal trapped in one, and he'd not been strong enough to free it. The suffering in that animal's eyes had seared his memory, and he'd made a vow to himself he'd never use such a heartless tool to do a job that, while never pleasant, could be done more humanely.

A flash of movement out of the corner of his eye caught Harry's attention. He froze, his senses on alert. The crack of old branches and the swish of ferns gently brushing up along the side of something large reached his ears. It might have been deer—possibly—but the gentle clinking sound that accompanied it quickly ruled out the possibility for Harry. Rather, it was the sound of someone trying to be quiet—and failing horribly. A thief. A poacher perhaps. Or even a game-keeper from another estate. All of them horrible at their chosen vocations if they made that much noise trundling in the woods. Either way, he didn't want any more trouble than he was already in.

He ducked behind the thick trunk of an ash, his fingers gripping the rough bark, his body tightening as a second wave of movement caught Harry's attention, coming from the opposite direction. This was quieter, almost more preda-tory. Dangerous. Lifting himself away from the tree so he would not rub against the bark and increase the chances of alerting anyone to his presence, he carefully turned to assess the danger. It took but a moment for him to find it. Before him was a game of cat and mouse—the cat armed with a throwing knife he was poised to let fly into the unsuspecting mouse who had a pistol in his hand, pointed in a different direction.

Without thinking, Harry swung the bolas once over his head and let it fly. The whoosh of the rope cut through the air, wrapping around the arm of the knife-wielding gentle-man. The whip of the cord and the force of the stones cut into him, dislodging the knife and eliciting a cry of pain and a string of words in a foreign tongue. The noise brought the attention of a second gentleman, who turned and shot. The man was dead before he hit the ground.

"Bloody hell," the man said, his voice gruff. Though he kept his expression neutral, his green-gray eyes were piercing.

Harry's hands were raised, and the two stood motionless as they appraised each other. The man with the pistol was older than Harry by decade, and a gentleman for certain. While he was dressed simply enough, his frock coat was made of a very fine brown wool, and his boots looked to be of the finest leather. Harry had the distinct and uncomfortable impression the gentleman was ingesting a thousand tiny details about him, details that would be tucked away like notes in the pockets of the gentleman's finely tailored coat.

"I know you," the gentleman said, lowering his weapon and returning it to a holsters at his side. "You're one of Whitmore's men. From the shoot. That's twice in nearly as many weeks you've saved my neck."

Harry nodded, placing him after a few moments. The gentleman had nearly found himself on the receiving end of a rifle full of birdshot, thanks to one of Viscount Whitmore's other guests.

"The name's Hamilton," the man continued. "Sir Richard Hamilton."

Harry gestured to the corpse. "Who was he?"

"A Spanish agent," Hamilton said, looking down at the man with disgust, then rummaged through his pockets. He pulled out a small folded sheaf of papers, examined them quickly, then tucked it away his own coat.

"You're a spy?" Harry said, incredulously. "You don't move like one."

Hamilton looked at him with mild disdain. "I admit that my natural habitat is a little less...natural. But you've done your king quite a service here, Mr..."

"Harry Boxford," he said, then retrieved his bolas from around the dead man's arm. "Good day to you."

The man's eyes narrowed. "How did you escape the tower at Langdon Park?"

Harry stiffened, ready to bolt. The man could have easily have a second firearm at his side, and from what Harry had already seen, whatever lack of skill he had making his way quietly in the woods, he more than made up for with his aim.

Sir Richard shook his head, gesturing with one hand to wave off his concerns.

"I make it my business to know things, Mr. Boxford. Like the fact that Sharpton is an extremely ill-tempered, peevish man who makes up for his shortcomings by bullying those around him. He also cheats at cards," Sir Richard said, "though be damned if I could convince Whitmore of it. Sharpton must have plenty on him if he's willing to toss his daughter away so carelessly."

Harry recalled Sara's determination to keep the family secrets at all cost. It was a rule she'd learned from her father, it seemed.

"Sharpton's a mean-spirited bastard," Harry said.

"He's more than that," Sir Richard said, his expression growing serious. "Lady Sara would be his second wife. His first met with an unfortunate...accident."

Hunger and fatigue were forgotten. Harry tensed, ready to run the ten miles back to Langdon Park in his bare feet.

"Come," Sir Richard said, motioning to Harry. "You have done more than your fair share of saving my skin. I must return the favor."

"Then I need a horse," Harry said. "And the other pistol I'm sure you have hidden in your coat."

"You are going no where alone. Sharpton will shoot you on sight." Sir Richard's eyes narrowed. "You won't have to worry about a rope, Boxford. Unless you are hell bent on getting yourself killed. You will trip over your own feet in those boots."

Harry looked down at his laceless boots.

"I will risk it," he said. "I would risk everything for Lady Sara. She can't be allowed to face this alone."

"I appreciate your bravery, Boxford, but you don't have to be so hell bent on doing this alone." Sir Richard adjusted his hat. "If you want my help, you will have it on my terms."

Harry raked a hand through his hair. "I will here them because I don't have a choice."

Sir Richard's lips curved in a shrew grin. "I do have a horse—two in fact. I also have a spare clean shirt. And soap. Just because you carry off the rough and ready look doesn't mean the lady wouldn't be happy to see you looking a little less...rugged. Besides, you deprived me of a good fight. I think I might be raring for another to take its place."

Harry crossed his arms, wary.

"Why are you helping me?"

"You've saved my neck twice, Harry Boxford. There are very few people on this earth who can claim that honor. I think it's in my best interests to keep you alive."

"You called for me, Father?"

Sara stood at the door of her father's study, her spine ramrod straight, her stomach clenched so tight she might have swallowed a lead ball. Physically and emotionally spent after a sleepless night, she'd gathered her reserves to bolster her courage for this moment. She'd spent most of the night packing a small trunk of her most prized possessions. She would make for London and throw herself on the mercy of the Baron and Baroness D'Anville. It was risky, but no less risky than what Harry had done for her. She had to save herself.

Her father sat at his desk, immersed in whatever problems the ledgers in front of him presented. Problems for which her marriage to Lord Sharpton was the remedy.

"Word has reached me that the prisoner has escaped," he said, his words clipped with undisguised anger. He cast a glare at Sara so sharp it could have cut steel. "But, I also suspect this is not a surprise."

Sara swallowed. She'd known there was a price that must be paid.

"He was an innocent man."

"He is a criminal." He rose, his chair pushed back hastily, a thunderous expression coming over his face. "A criminal you visited not once, but twice. Alone."

"Only to bring him food. He was locked up there to starve."

"Are you certain that is the only thing you served him?" He looked down at her with disgust. "Or did you lift your skirts like a common whore?"

A cold fury washed over Sara, hardening her. Her fingers curled into fists at her sides.

"The only person whoring in this room is you, Father. You're the one who sold your lands and your daughter to Lord Sharpton for a game of chance."

His eyes widened, his words coming out in a low growl. "You disgraceful wretch. How dare you speak to me this way," he spat, his cheeks flushed from his fury. "I am your father. I am—"

"A man grasping the remaining scraps of his dignity by selling his daughter," she said, traitorous tears pricking her eyes. From this moment on, not her father, not Lord Sharpton, not gaming wagers—would rule her. "You will never again lecture me on matters of behavior. No one in this house will ever lecture me again about anything."

The two stood silent.

"Lord Sharpton will send his men scouring the lands for him." A smile that was little more than sneer teased his lips. "If he's not dead already, he will be."

Sara took a deep breath, then relaxed. Harry had at least a twelve hour start.

"Harry Boxford is no longer my concern," she said. It was a lie, of course. She knew there would not be a day where she did not think about him. But this moment was about her welfare. And except for Harry, no one else had been concerned about her. "I will not marry Lord Sharpton. He can have Langdon Park and whatever else you promised in that gaming hell. But he cannot have me."

Her father's eyes narrowed.

"You do not get to decide that," he said. "Lord Sharpton is a man of consequence! And you have repaid his condescension with such vile, disgraceful behavior. You should be glad he stooped to marry such a horse-faced cunt."

The base vulgarity of her father's words knocked Sara back a step as if he'd pushed her. But instead of hot fury, a cold sensation came over her, numbing her pain. It sharpened her senses, allowing her to see for the first time, the truth of her surroundings. The façade of civility, of superiority this man...of the estate...crumbled away. Not even the smartest brocade coat or shiniest buckles on his shoes could hide the baseness before her.

Know your worth, her grandmother had once told her. And in the past few days she had discovered it.

"Once I would have believed he was worthy," she said. "But I had not yet met anyone who'd lived up to that quality. I only had you."

A stinging slap to her cheek was her father's reply. He gripped her arm as he screamed for his butler. Sara tried to pull away, but his hold only tightened. Soon she found herself fighting two burly footmen who dragged her back to her bedchamber and tossed her inside. She stumbled backward, vaguely aware of her father's vehemence and hateful curses as the door closed behind her, locked from the other side with a click.

"Father!"

"You will be married in the morning if I have to drag you to the altar myself."

Sara paced to the door, pulling on it until her hands were sore. After a short while, her fury subsided to a moment of exasperation at her own short-sightedness. She should have anticipated that a man desperate enough to bet his estate would be desperate enough to keep her from escaping at all costs.

She went to the window. The ground was perhaps twenty feet below her. Too high to jump. There had to be another way. If she was smart enough to get Harry what he needed to get out of the Old Tower, surely to heaven she could manage it for herself. Quietly she picked up the chair from her dressing table and nestled it under the door handle, to ensure entry into the room would be more difficult. She gripped the covers from her bed, pulled off the sheets, and rummaged through her sewing basket for her scissors, methodically cutting them in thirds. Sara knotted the ends together, and when it was clear there was not quite enough length, she sliced up some of her bed curtains as well.

When she was finished, she tucked the scissors back in her little sewing kit, and placed it in the bag she had packed last evening. There was enough coins and jewelry to get her to London, and if things truly went awry, to lease a room for a time. If she was diligent, perhaps she could find work as a seamstress. It would be hard work, but it was her life. And she would find a way to live it. It was an exhilarating and terrifying feeling.

She had just finished tying one end of her makeshift rope to the edge of the bed when the heavy sounds of footfalls caught her attention. Someone was coming. She threw open the window and tossed the remainder of the rope out the window, watching its length unfurl until it hit the ground. She tossed her bag after it.

The sound of a key scraping into the lock sent her heart thrumming in her chest, and any fear she had about taking the first step out the window were overridden by the sound of someone struggling to open the door.

"Sara!"

Her father's strangled cry rose above the pounding. Without another thought, she wrapped the linen rope around her arms and slowly lowered herself over the window.

Don't look down, she said to herself over and over again. She'd loosened her stays, but the sleeves of her dress made it difficult to keep her arms above her head and she felt them start to tear. Fear rose in her chest, and she fought to breathe as her body swayed on the line. Above her, she could hear the pounding get louder. Around her, a stiff summer wind brushed across her face as the sun started to lower. *Don't look down.*

Bracing her feet against the side of the stone, she lowered the hand closest to the ground, then brought the upper one down to meet it. Forcing herself to think about nothing else but this one thing, she repeated this motion over and over. Her arms were shaking from exertion.

"Sara."

The sound of her name, coming from below caught her off guard. The voice was heartbreakingly familiar, though the sound of her name on that tongue was not. Was she being driven made by desperation, or was it…Harry?

"Sara, listen to me. I'm going to get you down, but you must listen carefully."

Harry's calm measured voice was like a balm to her heart, and it was all she could do not to cry.

"Weave the rope between your feet. Catch the rope with the top of one foot and lower the other so your feet are together. Then keep them tightly together. Can you do that?"

Sara squeezed her eyes shut and tried to manipulate her feet. It took every last ounce of her strength to manage it, but after three tries she was able to make it work.

"I have it!" she called back, unable to keep the fear out of her voice.

"Good! Now that is going to act as a stopper to keep you from going too fast. You are going to loosen your hands, just a bit each time, squeezing your feet hard to keep you from sliding down too quickly," he said. "Can you do that?"

"I don't know!" she yelled out.

"I do."

Could she? Panic kept her in place until the sound of a large bang, like the explosion of a pistol shot, rang out from above her. A moment later, she looked up and her father and Lord Sharpton were above her, the latter with a murderous look in his eye.

She couldn't look up anymore. Sara squeezed her feet together, and loosened her hands ever so slightly. For a terrifying moment she thought she was going to fall, but using her feet as an anchor she was able to slowly, in jerky movements, move toward the ground. She could do this.

She was but ten feet from the ground when, to her horror, she caught a glimpse of Lord Sharpton running toward them, drawing his pistol.

"Harry!"

"Let go, my lady," she heard Harry say from beneath her. "I will catch you."

CHAPTER 13

Sara looked down to see Harry, his arms outstretched, reaching for her. He was at once tantalizingly in reach, and yet...it still seemed so far to the ground.

"Let go," he repeated, his voice calm, his smile gifting her with confidence. "Let go and this will all be over."

She nodded, then let go, only to find herself cradled in his arms. Harry squeezed her tight against him. They still had to run, but now they could do it together.

"Let's hurry this along, shall we?"

Harry set her down, and Sara turned to see a gentleman—Sir Richard Hamilton, of all people—holding a pistol over the body of Lord Sharpton, who was flat on his back, apparently unconscious.

There was no time for asking why Sir Richard was training a gun on the viscount, or how Harry had managed to find his way back to her. Harry grabbed her by her hand, scooped up her bag, and they bolted toward the horse. He mounted the beast and pulled her up in front with her belongings tucked in her lap. His arms around her, he clicked the reins and the two bolted, Hamilton behind them.

She had expected to ride through the night. Instead, they'd gone only a few miles before Sir Richard, now ahead, led them down what appeared to be a small cattle path. It twisted and turned until Sara could no longer tell which way they had come. At last, they arrived at a small hunting lodge.

"What is this place?" she asked.

"Refuge, my lady—for the night at least," Harry replied, easing her off the horse. Beside them, Sir Richard dismounted.

"Thank you for helping us," she said to him, her heart still pounding from all that had happened. "But I don't understand why."

"Quite simple really," Sir Richard began, gesturing toward Harry. "He has proven himself quite useful to me. I thought I should repay the favor." His mouth quirked a little, before turning to Harry. "What happens next is up to you. In the meantime, I will make sure the area is secure, and then, I trust, we shall have a toast? Heaven knows I need a brandy."

Sara watched him walk away, then turned to Harry, who was watching her intently.

"I thought you were gone," she said, her voice shaking.

"I found my own company wanting. And I could never really leave you," he replied, smiling at her so earnestly Sara thought her heart would burst. He took her hands and placed them on his chest. She could feel the strong steady thrumming of his heart. "I had a piece of you here. And maybe I'm a selfish man, but it wasn't enough. I needed the rest of you."

"I am glad you are selfish." She laughed through the happiest of tears. "I believe I am equally so."

Sara threw herself into his arms and buried her head in his chest, hugging him as if she feared him leaving her. Though she knew in her heart that he never would.

"What do we do now?" she asked. "My father and Lord Sharpton will never stop looking for us."

"I am learning that life is easier when you aren't hell bent on distrusting everyone you encounter," he said. "This cottage is a safe refuge. We can remain here for several days. I have secured some work at an estate in Warwickshire. A gentleman has come into an Earldom and needs a game-keeper. Sir Richard has promised me a strong letter of recommendation."

"Harry, how have you accomplished all this in one day?" Indeed, he'd washed, had on a fresh change of clothing and even a new pair of boots. Not that he wasn't handsome before. But he stood a little straighter now. As if he finally realized he was the man she'd always believed him to be. "Did you get yourself a guardian angel?"

"It seems I have become a guardian angel," he said, gesturing to the lodge where Sir Richard was waiting.

"You have always been mine."

Harry took her by the hands. "My lady, I—"

"I like it better when you call me Sara," she said, rising up on her toes, and brushing her lips against his. A winding heat rose in her body, her fingers wrapping around the back of his neck. She breathed in deeply, taking in Harry's scent, a small sigh escaping her as Harry's tongue slipped between her lips. He pulled her close, and she opened her mouth wider, hungrily answering his kisses with her own.

"I love you, Sara," he said at last, breaking the kiss, his voice low with a need that matched her own. "With all my heart."

"What do we do now?" she said.

"We can make for Warwickshire. It is far enough away that we should escape Lord Sharpton's notice," he said, holding her face his in hands. "Though I'd hoped we would make a small side trip to Scotland. If you wish, Sara."

Sara squeezed his hands in hers. "Scotland? To marry?"

He nodded. "To Gretna Green. My father was a blacksmith. I thought...we could..." He swallowed deeply. "That is, if you would wish it. I would never force you to do anything you didn't want to."

Tears streamed down Sara's face. She had no home. She wealth except for the few jewels she'd managed to bring with her. She had no one except Harry Boxford. And she could never recall being happier or more complete than she had at this moment.

"My grandmother once told me I would marry an honorable man. And I will, when I marry you."

Harry put a gentle kiss to her forehead, then folded her hands into his, his brow creased by doubt.

"Are you certain? Your life will not be easy, Sara. I wish on my life I could give you the comforts you are accustomed to," he said. "But I promise on my life to honor you, and love you, and give you everything that I am."

"The only comfort I require is you." She took his fingers to his mouth, and peppered them with small kisses, before reaching up and cupping the side of his face with her hand. She was nervous for their future, but she was not scared. "My future now has hope. It has possibility. And it has love. I could not wish for more."

The low rumble of thunder came from the distance, and the skies darkened.

"Come." Sir Richard's slightly irritated call from the door of the cottage rose over the approaching storm. "I can't toast the happy couple if you are out here. I need my brandy after a day like I've had."

"He's a grumpy guardian angel, but he's ours," Sara said, overcome by a sense that nothing, not even the loudest thunder nor the darkest cloud could ruin the intense sense of joy running through her body. "And you are mine."

"Yes, my lady."

"Harry," Sara tapped Harry playfully on his shoulder, then took his hand, leading him to the cottage. "I am quite finished with being called 'my lady'."

Harry's eyes darkened ever so slightly, and he lowered his voice in a way that threatened to bewitch Sara entirely.

"If I might be so bold," he replied, "you will soon be *my* lady. But perhaps you would prefer another title?"

Sara pressed a kiss to the tender skin behind his ear.

"I believe Mrs. Boxford would do nicely."

A few drops started to fall out of the sky, and Sara let out a whoop as Harry scooped her up and started toward shelter, then paused before stepping over the threshold.

"Yes, my love."

THE END

A NOTE FROM THE AUTHOR

I hope you enjoyed **No Place for a Lady**. This novella is a prequel to my *Enchanted Tales* Series. Enchanted Tales are all historical romances with a Fairy Tale twist. Fairy Tales have some of my favourite, timeless themes, and I love playing with them. I hope you enjoy reading them too.

If you're new to the series, introduce yourself to Stephen Pembroke in **Not Your Average Beauty**, a melancholy marquess who needs a brilliant bookworm to break through his curse. I've included the first chapter so you can take a peak!

Reviews are welcome - and super important to indie authors, and helpful to readers as well, so you if can leave a review, I'd be super grateful! Feel free to post one where you purchased the book, or on Goodreads.

My website is www.michellehelliwell.com, and you'll find me on Facebook and Instagram as well. Join my mailing list and get a heads up on new releases, and special giveaways that are only for my subscribers.

NOT YOUR AVERAGE BEAUTY

CHAPTER 1

Yorkshire, October 1790

There was blood on his hands.

Who—or what—it belonged to, he didn't know. His temples pounded as he attempted to drag himself up onto his bed. He lifted a shaking hand, sticky and stinking of the drying blood, to his brow, but the act brought the putrid smell too close to his nose. Already weakened, his stomach lurched in protest, and he heaved violently onto the floor.

Glorious. Just bloody glorious.

Was it not but a fortnight ago he'd subjected himself to another session of incomprehensible incantations and bitter potions by a so-called magician? More money and time wasted. And, perhaps, one more thread of hope unraveled in his never ending quest to be free of the Beast. Priests and scholars, alchemists and magicians from every corner of Europe and even beyond had been consulted. No distance had been too far, nor any price demanded too high. For the cost of this horror—waking up in a soup of filth and blood, causing terror among the people it was his duty to protect—was higher still.

The jangle of keys in the lock of his bedchamber door announced help was on its way. In the next instant his butler Hanley, who had served his father before him, entered the room, bringing relief along with a heavy dose of humiliation. He was vaguely aware of Hanley's calm and measured voice directing the small parade of house staff that dared to remain in his employ. They took care of the mess as if cleaning up after a dinner party. As he was hauled up onto his bed and a warm cloth brought to his face, he silently made a note to talk to his steward about giving Hanley a raise in his salary.

Gripped by thirst, he lunged for the jug brought for washing, pulled it out of the hands of the young and no doubt terrified maid, and gulped it down. He motioned for more, and only after he downed another, did he feel sated in any way.

Only after his ablutions and a cup of the blackest coffee, soundly fortified with whiskey, could Stephen Pembroke, Marquess of Pembroke, finally focus on his surroundings. His footmen righted the armoire, and the maids cleared away the bloodied bedclothes and scurried away. The broken mirror, the tenth he'd smashed over the years, was picked up and his room brought back to some sort of order. Between mirrors and broken windows, if there was no one else in the area pleased about the Beast of Barronsfield; the local glazier was no doubt grateful for the business.

"Hanley," Stephen managed to croak at last. Despite the water he had drunk, his throat was like dust.

"My lord?"

"Do you know…?" God, how he hated asking this. "Have you heard—"

"The vicarage," the butler began, then cleared his throat, pausing long enough to let Stephen know there was more.

"Out with it man," Stephen barked. A stabbing pain forced him to close his eyes. He allowed it to pass, and let out a long breath, remembering some line about not shooting the messenger. "My apologies, Hanley. My head is pounding like the devil. Please, just tell me. Is anyone missing?"

"The vicar is missing most of his hen house, his dog—"

"Oh my God."

"I believe that is what the vicar said, my lord."

Mr. Darling, the vicar, owned a Scottish terrier who followed him happily around the village and was visitor and friend to the invalids and foundlings tended to at the small village infirmary. Stephen's lips twisted in disgust. How could he have killed such a harmless creature?

"Anything else?"

"That is all the news that has reached me, my lord."

A shallow relief set in, but he was entitled to none. It had been five years since the curse had claimed a human life. But it had. Long before his family curse had taken this darker, sinister turn, it had claimed five. There had been blood on his hands for years.

Gripping the side of his bed, Stephen forced himself onto his feet, then signaled for Hanley to help him get dressed. "Right. I will meet with the vicar to discuss compensation for his losses. Has Schofield returned?"

"Not yet, my lord."

"Send word I wish to speak with him as soon as he arrives." Stephen stood, his gaze fixed on the bedchamber door while Hanley tied Stephen's cravat to the butler's exacting standard. He felt like the devil, but he needed to look like a marquess, especially when he was about to go out among his tenants. After a few minutes of Hanley's fussing over collars and cuffs, Stephen waved the man off. He had a parson to speak to. Another set of wrongs to be righted. Another set of rumors to face. It had been months since the old woman's curse had reared its head, but he still felt unprepared for the horror of it. Stephen raked a shaky hand through his hair, and tried to collect himself. Tried to shake off the grip of the Beast.

It was becoming harder and harder to do.

ROSALIND SCHOFIELD HAD VISITED the bright blue waters and pink sand of Bermuda, and once—though she could barely remember it—the rolling tobacco fields of Virginia. But it had been sixteen years since she'd last visited England, and the winding journey from Devon to Yorkshire allowed her to become reacquainted with much of it. Her father, Captain John Schofield, had long promised to take her back, but it was a promise he kept only in death. Both he and his crew had been lost at sea in the North Atlantic. She'd left her late mother's sister and family in the colonies to come into the guardianship of her uncle and take possession of an inheritance that would give her a very comfortable living.

"I am sorry that our meeting is by way of John's passing—he was very proud of you, my girl. Very proud, and I can see why. You are a fine young woman, Rosalind," her uncle said, sitting opposite her in the well-sprung carriage spiriting them to her new home. His countenance reminded Rosalind so much of her father it both pained and comforted her. "I am glad to see you after all these months of waiting since the news." He paused then smiled. "Of course, the last time I saw you, you were naught but an imp, reaching no taller than the last button on my waistcoat."

"It is good to be with you, Uncle." A curious sort of joy bubbled inside her. The unfamiliar feeling begat quiet tears and a smile all at once. Her uncle's genuine pleasure in her company was a new experience. She'd lived most of her life in a bustling household in Halifax with her Aunt and Uncle

Stanhope and their three daughters, where there was plenty of company to be had, little of it amiable. Rosalind learned early that a crowded room could be a very lonely place, indeed.

"We are not long now from Barronsfield," her uncle continued in low, rumbling tones. "When we arrive, I will show you to your rooms, and leave you to rest and become acquainted with your new home. Later, if the mist clears, we can take a tour of the grounds, if you so wish."

"I would very much, thank you." She saw the nervousness in his eyes, and reached forward to take his hand. Having a niece to care for, even if she was a grown woman, was new for her uncle, and probably just as nerve-wracking as learning of the death of a beloved brother.

"Barronsfield is one of the most beautiful estates in all of England, and the steward's cottage is very comfortable. I think you will be well pleased with it." Her uncle brightened as he spoke. "I had some assistance from Mrs. Darling, the vicar's wife, as to what would be suitable quarters for a young lady. In fact, she has invited you to the vicarage for tea tomorrow to meet some of the other ladies in the neighborhood. Some of the younger ones will be going on to London too, no doubt, once the season starts, so you will have something in common."

"I am looking forward to all of it." All except going to London. The idea of standing in a ballroom, being looked over—or worse, overlooked—did not appeal, especially at her age. Twenty-eight was well past the prime for having a season.

Rosalind had already spent far too much of her life with people who didn't truly care for her, and to be bound in marriage to one was hardly an appealing fate. Her inheritance had given her an unexpected choice. The large sum could fetch her attention she might not otherwise receive at her age, and a reasonable match. But if she didn't marry, by thirty she would inherit the total amount. She could travel, or own a nice cottage with a beautiful little library, and not have to tie herself to anyone. She settled further into the cushioned bench of the carriage and let out a little sigh. Two years was not so very long a time to wait.

The countryside rolled along, and beyond the stone hedges and fields, the trees were giving up their green color for fall's golden hues. Passing into Yorkshire, the landscape changed, growing wilder with every mile. Craggy rocks and fields abundant with soft heather met a sky that seemed to have reached down from the heavens to touch it. Eventually, rolling fog and mist enveloped the landscape. Occasionally she could make out the ghost of a lone tree in the miasma, and it felt like she was on the road to some otherworldly place.

The carriage lumbered on until it reached the market town of Elmsdale. Thick gray clouds blanketed the tops of the stone and wooden buildings built in the time of Elizabeth. It was similar in appearance to many of the villages they'd already passed, and yet something about it left Rosalind a little disquieted. Lonely signs hung from deserted shop fronts, creaking on ancient iron hinges. Windows were shuttered, and the only sound was the rumbling of the carriage wheels on the cobblestone square.

A quick study of Uncle Reginald's face told her something was amiss. The pink that had colored his cheeks a moment ago had disappeared, leaving a pallor that matched his graying beard.

Ahead, the steeple of an old stone church pierced the mist. Past the church was what looked like a parsonage, where a large group of men had gathered, clearly agitated. Her uncle pounded the top of the carriage with his walking stick, and Rosalind lurched in her seat as they came to an abrupt stop.

"Please stay here, my dear," he said. "I shan't be long." Without giving her the chance to protest, he hopped out of the carriage and was immediately accosted by a rough sort of man, younger than her uncle by perhaps a decade.

"Coming to check out your master's handiwork?" the stranger jeered.

"I have no idea what you're talking about, Tom."

"Don't you start your blubbering with me. We know something is up—something evil, and we mean to do something about it, see?"

Rosalind peered out the window, catching her uncle's gaze. He started walking away from the carriage, but he was soon surrounded by several others who were far too threatening for Rosalind's liking. Her hackles rising, she jumped out of the carriage. A damp breeze wafted a putrid odor in her direction. Overcoming the assault on her senses, she strained to make out the worried, angry voices talking over one another.

The approaching thunder of hoof falls silenced the crowd. Seconds later, a huge black horse appeared, coming to a halt near the gathering. Two dozen heads turned in unison to the rider, who dismounted and strode in among the villagers. The man was taller than her uncle by several inches, and the breadth of his shoulders gave him a commanding presence. His hair, tied back in a hasty queue, was the color of straw in an August sun, contrasting with the heavy, black, woolen cape that hung about his shoulders. A flutter stirred in her belly and she abandoned propriety to strain her neck to get a closer look.

Her uncle immediately went to him. If Uncle Reginald was unnerved by whatever had happened here, he hid it well.

"My Lord Barronsfield."

"Schofield," the rider acknowledged. Rosalind studied the man who she knew from her uncle was his employer, the Marquess of Barronsfield.

The marquess spoke calmly with the vicar, who appeared anything but as he motioned wildly to the carcasses of fowl strewn over the yard and the remains of what looked to be a small poultry house. The upset on the man's long, gaunt face was clear, even at this distance. She tried to pick out the man who'd been so angry with her uncle a moment ago, but there was too much frantic activity to focus on any one person.

"—six geese and at least a dozen chickens."

"—last night. Horrible howling sound. Chilled me bones, it did."

"—heard young Jack Gates saw the whole thing, 'cept he's too scared to talk."

The discordant voices continued unabated. She shook her head. What manner of beast could have caused such destruction and sparked such fear among men of hardy farming stock?

"Gentlemen," the marquess called out with an unmistakable air of authority, and the din quickly settled. The crowd was silent, but the expressions on their faces spoke volumes.

Rosalind watched the marquess as he listened with what seemed like genuine interest to the vicar's tale. The village men were appraising his actions as well, some obviously approving of the way the marquess confronted the ordeal, though far more were hanging back, clearly undecided.

"I assure you this will be dealt with to your satisfaction, Mr. Darling." He shook hands with the vicar, who seemed to have calmed somewhat.

"Our wives are scared, your Lordship." The voice came from the crowd, and several men stepped aside to let one from their ranks take center stage. The man, who looked to be a farmer, removed his cap and took what Rosalind felt for him to be a rather daring step forward. "Folks have been sayin' some horrible things 'bout what goes on at Barronsfield, my lord."

Horrible things? Rosalind stood a little straighter, cocking her head, doubting for a moment what she'd heard. Her uncle had yet to mention anything unusual about Barronsfield. And certainly nothing *horrible*.

"And what things might these be?"

"Just talk, your Lordship," the man said, daring to look the marquess in the eye.

"Look, Harrison," Lord Barronsfield replied, exasperation and fatigue in his voice. "I know you're frightened. There is no man more angry than I about this situation. Everyone should know there hasn't been a lord who dared to call himself the Marquess of Barronsfield who would let any harm come to his tenants or servants." Lord Barronsfield's voice rose above the crowd. "The truths and the falsehoods have all mingled to make this a murky tale, but I tell you Harrison, and every other soul under my protection, that I am doing everything within my power to end this." He put out his hand to the farmer, who took it after a brief hesitation. They exchanged a firm handshake, seemingly satisfying some of the men nearby.

After they were done, the marquess and her uncle started walking toward the carriage, deep in quiet conversation.

Eager not to be caught disobeying her uncle, Rosalind hopped back inside, straightened her skirts, then pulled on the door to shut it. Before she'd had the opportunity to let go of the latch, the door flew open, pulling her off-balance. Rather unceremoniously, she tumbled out of the carriage, landing on the graveled park with a thud.

"Oooh!"

Almost as quickly as she fell, she found herself pulled to her feet by a set of large hands.

"Are you hurt, my dear?" Her uncle asked.

She shook her head, dusted her skirts as best she could while trying to reclaim her dignity.

"Sorry, Uncle. Aunt Stanhope always said I wasn't the most graceful of creatures. I was hoping to prove her—"

"My dear," her uncle began, clearing his throat. "I have the great honor to introduce you to my employer and your host, Stephen Pembroke, sixth Marquess of Barronsfield. My lord, my niece, Miss Rosalind Schofield."

Rosalind's head snapped up, and she stifled a groan. Rosalind had imagined her eventual meeting with the marquess. She'd practiced what to say a thousand times on the journey to Yorkshire. She'd envisioned her graceful address. Yet here he stood, having just picked her off the ground while she prattled on unawares. Heat flushed into her cheeks.

She dipped quickly into what she hoped was the ladylike curtsey she had originally planned for this occasion. The marquess said nothing at first, but stood there, examining her as if she were a new species of cabbage.

Rosalind waited for him to say something—*anything*—to her. She clasped her fingers together and willed her herself still. She shouldn't have been so nervous, but then she'd never met someone of his rank before. This was the devil the townsfolk had spoken of? He looked to be an ordinary sort of man. Well, perhaps *ordinary* was not quite the right word for him. Handsome, more like. His eyes were an incredibly dark brown—nearly black in fact—with an intensity that might have been off-putting if not for the gentle line of his brow. His cheeks were ruddied, and there was a haggardness to him that was unexpected for a man of his stature, yet it leant an air of wildness she found at once appealing and a little dangerous.

"Thank you for letting me stay with my uncle, my lord. It

is very generous," she said at last as she tried to control her nervousness.

"Think nothing of it, Miss Schofield," he replied. "Allow me to extend my condolences to you on the loss of your father."

"Thank you," she said, surprised he would stoop to comment on her circumstances.

An uncomfortable silence followed. Every rustle of fabric, every shuffle of boots over the dirt begged for a response. Rosalind's mind raced for something to say, but nothing of consequence was forthcoming.

He pressed his lips together, giving Rosalind the impression he wished to be miles away. Gone was the easy manner present when he spoke with the men in the village, or any hint of the smile she saw when he spoke with her uncle a few moments ago. He was guarded, and even a tad awkward. The tension stretching across his brow suggested he was suffering some discomfort.

"Are you cold, Miss Schofield?" he said at last.

"No, my lord," Rosalind replied, confused.

She cast a glance over to her uncle who casually bounced once or twice on his toes, then with the slightest of nods, gestured to her feet. Rosalind, embarrassed, took the hint. She hadn't realized she'd been bouncing on her toes, an old habit she'd tried without success to banish. "My apologies, my lord. The journey has been long. I can be a horrible fidget when I am forced to sit for any great length of time."

"I was extolling the beauty of Barronsfield on the journey. She is quite eager to explore the grounds, and the village as well," her uncle said.

"Especially the bookshop," she continued, her nerves taking over, speeding up her speech. "I probably should not own to it, but I adore novels and fairy tales, though I suppose they have the admirable quality of keeping me still."

"No Fordyce's Sermons, or Mrs. Chapone's Letters?" the marquess asked.

"Heavens no. I have tried, you see, but then I fidget even more."

His only reply was a smile, but Rosalind caught something in his face that took her breath away. And then, as magically as it appeared, it disappeared.

A whiff of not-so-freshly killed hen brought her back to the mess around her. Trampled feathers littered the damp ground. A flash of brown fabric nearly escaped her notice in the hardening muck. Removing her glove, she bent and pulled the object out of the ground.

"What is that?" the marquess asked.

"I'm not certain. It looks to be a reticule, though a very modest one. Perhaps it belongs to the vicar's wife?"

The marquess motioned to her uncle. "Schofield, perhaps this might be useful to your investigation?"

"Here my dear," her uncle took the mud soaked purse. "I will inquire with Mr. Darling." He exchanged an uneasy glance with Lord Barronsfield before leaving to find the vicar.

Rosalind returned to her scrutiny of the trampled ground, and scrunched her brow in concentration "Do the authorities have any idea of who or what did this?"

The marquess started, surveying her with a new interest. "You have not heard of me."

"I don't—"

"Interesting." The tension in his brow lifted, and something approaching a smile teased his mouth. "Very interesting."

Confused, she cast a glance over each shoulder then back to Lord Barronsfield. His hands were on his hips, his dark gaze fixed on her. Swallowing deeply, she tried to ignore the excitement rising in her chest and push aside any idea that she might be the object of his attention. Feelings like that only ended in disappointment. Luckily, her uncle returned before she could allow herself to be distracted by them.

"My lord, if you would permit me, I will see my niece home and then return to assist with the clean up," her uncle said.

"Of course, Schofield," the marquess said. "I do not wish to delay your journey further, Miss Schofield."

"I hope the villain will be found."

The marquess's mouth hardened into a line. "I assure you, the villain is paying for his crimes." He bowed politely. "I bid you good-day."

Rosalind watched the marquess mount his horse and ride off until he disappeared down the road. A lightness carried her steps as she climbed into the carriage. She settled in, smiling at nothing in particular until she caught sight of the worried look on her uncle's brow as he took his seat opposite her. He smiled, but distress kept the joy from reaching his eyes. The carriage moved along as before, but silence was no longer easy. She had a dozen questions for him.

"Uncle," she said at last, no longer able to contain her worry. "I could not help but notice the rough manner with which some of the villagers were treating you."

"Pay no mind to that, my dear." He shuffled on the bench. "'Tis nothing but the foolish superstitions of simpletons, fueled by bad luck and ale."

The obvious false bravery her uncle put forth didn't make her feel any better. "Does his lordship know?"

"Heavens no, Rosalind. My dear, you must understand. The marquess is a very important man. Now, let's get you home and think of more pleasant matters, shall we?" With that, he continued on about the details of her new parlor as if nothing unpleasant had happened. Rosalind chose to relax and allow herself to be swept up in her uncle's enthusiasm once more. But somewhere in the back of her mind, the threatening voice from behind the carriage lingered.

So did the marquess's intoxicating gaze, a look laced with sadness. She shook her head, chiding herself for even daring to give him a second thought. Though he was flesh and blood, she had a better chance with a mythical prince from one of her books. Or a fortune hunter. That would surely be her fate in London, where a plain girl with a good dowry might find marriage, but not love.

Better to have no marriage at all.

THOUGH THE MORNING fog had dissipated by the time Stephen returned his mount to the stables, the gloom was more reflective of his mood. What a mess. He'd forced himself to stand still when Mr. Darling showed him the broken body of his beloved little terrier, even while it tore at Stephen's insides. And when he heard about Jack Gates, a stone had dropped in his gut. From what Stephen could discover, the lad was hurt, but would recover. Another night like this and even the most loyal of his tenants might turn their backs on him.

Walking across the fields of his estate, the small meandering lane that led to the steward's cottage caught his attention. After years of absolute loyalty and dedication, it was very little for him to grant Schofield the favor of allowing his niece to stay at the cottage with him. But after this morning, he wondered if Schofield might change his mind.

He strode past the rose gardens, their blossoms long spent, thinking about the girl who had traipsed through the Darling's poultry yard, her skirts rumpled from travel. That unceremonious exit from the carriage onto his boots pulled his mouth into a smile every time he reflected on it. He hadn't spent much time around women in the past five years, but Miss Schofield was undoubtedly one of the more unconventional ladies he'd met. Unconventional was fine, but beauty was another matter. Beauty, he had discovered even as a boy, was dangerous for him. And far more dangerous for the ones he'd dared to love.

Miss Schofield would be safe from the Beast's curse. She was neither too short nor too tall. Her figure was pleasant enough; she wasn't thin, nor was she overly plump. Her complexion was neither drab nor brilliant; she had a light sprinkling of freckles across her nose that some might consider charming. Her eyes appeared unable to make up their mind as to color; at one moment they attempted blue, then seemed to settle on a greenish-gray. Her hair was not golden, like Catherine's, neither was it raven black like Anne's. Rather it was a shade of non-descript brown, worn back in the conventional fashion.

She was, without a doubt, one of the plainest girls he had ever seen. She lacked title and privilege and she was perhaps a few years older than the ideal, though still young enough to bear him an heir. At one time he might have been more particular, but he was running out of time. He was willing to forgo his scruples on that point. Barronsfield needed an heir.

He needed the most unremarkable woman he could find. And here she was.

There were no fireworks, no arrows to the heart, no rapturous pangs of any kind, nor even the hint of a note from a choir of angels singing above proclaiming she was "the one." His breath did not catch in his throat at the sight of her, nor did he feel his palms tingle when he picked her up off the ground.

Still, her smile was pleasant. Nothing that set him into raptures, but warm, and even comforting. She spoke as if she had a brain in her head, which might make for pleasant conversation. By the ease of her manner with him, it was clear she was unaware she was speaking to the Beast of Barronsfield, or that such a creature even existed. It had shocked him into silence, and opened him up to the possibility that he would not lose Barronsfield after all.

Yes. She would do. Buoyed by hope, Stephen raced back to the manor, quite certain he could shortly have this whole marriage business neatly sewn up.

By tomorrow.

NOT YOUR AVERAGE BEAUTY

When beauty is a curse, only love can break the spell

Stephen Pembroke, the Marquess of Barronsfield, believes that where his love of beauty goes, death follows. Cursed to a loveless existence, and with his legacy at stake, Stephen makes a desperate proposal of marriage to Rosalind Schofield, his steward's new ward - and the plainest girl he has ever met. Rosalind has spent a lifetime being overlooked for prettier faces. When she is singled out for her lack of beauty by the Marquess, she begins to doubt if she is deserving of the love she inwardly craves.

When unusual things start happening around her, Rosalind can't help but wonder if Lord Barronsfield or his curse are who and what they appear to be. When she openly challenges Stephen about the curse, he begins to doubt everything – and comes to realize that this apparently plain, ordinary woman is not as unremarkable as he believed. Strange things *are* happening in Barronsfield. As they move closer to the truth, Rosalind unwittingly finds herself in the sights of the real beast in Barronsfield, and Stephen must decide if his growing love for Rosalind will be his salvation or her doom.

Get the Book

NO PRINCE CHARMING (ENCHANTED TALES #2)

Love is the fairest of them all

Dashing off in a daring elopement with a prince handpicked by her mother, Lady Gwyneth Snowdon anticipates a lavish future. But when a mysterious stranger kidnaps her, Gwyneth fears her happy ending is doomed.

Used by his maniacal father, Edmund Pembroke turned his back on society. Seizing the opportunity to say good-bye to his past forever, he makes a deal to separate the pampered countess from a gold-digging imposter. But when Edmund discovers her life is in danger, he is forced to protect the beautiful, well-born Gwyneth Snowdon and to confront his ghosts.

Separated from her plush surroundings, Gwyneth learns she's capable of so much—including love for a man with neither title nor fortune. But she begins to suspects there is more to her rugged, handsome guardian than he's chosen to reveal. After finding herself at the center of a sinister deception, can she dare to trust her heart to a man who's spent years deceiving himself?

Get the Book

NEVER TRUST A ROGUE IN WOLF'S CLOTHING (ENCHANTED TALES #3)

A heart all the better to love her with

After three torturous seasons, Lady Eleanore Pembroke is finished with husband hunting and happy ever after. Following the scandal of a broken engagement, eager to bury herself in her work at the local infirmary, she returns home shocked to discover their trusted physician gone, replaced by a dashing scoundrel. Bastien DuMont is a talented doctor, but Eleanore senses his restless heart. She's no longer prepared to risk hers, nor the trust of the people who've come to depend on him.

Caught up in a revolution that dissolved into terror, Bastien learned that devotion is for fools. On the run from a growing list of men who'd love to see him dead, he's forced out of the shadows and into the shoes of a respectable country physician, putting him under the scrutiny of Lady Eleanore, a local do-gooder immune to his roguish charms. When a mysterious figure emerges, threatening his life and the safety of those around him, can Bastien hunt down his opponent before he becomes the prey? Or is exposing his heart the greater danger?

Get the Book

NOTHING MAGICAL ABOUT MIDNIGHT (ENCHANTED TALES #4)

When hearts seek out their perfect fit, love transforms us all

Kitty Boxford isn't the sort of girl that gets invited to the ball of the century, but she has other plans to find herself a husband. The very serious but oh-so handsome Marquess of Ellsworth needs an assistant for his observatory, and it's the perfect opportunity to earn the money she needs to hatch her husband-hunting plan. What isn't in her plans is to fall in love with a Duke-in-waiting...someone as out of reach as the stars.

For Colin Middleton, Lord Ellsworth, his scientific endeavors have been the distraction for his broken heart, not the bevy of ladies his marriage-minded parents have invited for a grand ball. When a gamekeeper's daughter demands the job as his assistant, he initially discounts her as far too unqualified and far too female for the job. But the alluring Miss Boxford is more than just an excellent assistant, and there is nothing logical about the way she makes him feel. Still, there is a formula for marriage in the peerage...and marrying a gamekeeper's daughter is not part of the equation.

When Colin's father becomes ill, the pressure to take his place in the family – with an appropriate bride and the requisite heirs – mounts. Logically, Kitty is the last woman he should want to marry. But there's nothing logical about love...

Get the Book

ABOUT THE AUTHOR

Michelle Helliwell started writing her first novel, a time travel fantasy, when she was 15. She moved on to half-hearted attempts at something more literary, then nearly gave up on the writing all together until one fine day in 2005 a co-worker put a romance novel in her hands and told her to "get over yourself".

She did, and the rest, as they say, is history.

Michelle lives with her husband and two sons in Nova Scotia, Canada where moody weather and bagpipes are plentiful, but alas, guys in puffy shirts are too few.

Connect with me online!
www.michellehelliwell.com

9 781999 496579